Nutcracker
and
Mouse King

E.T.A. Hoffmann

CLASSICS

Published 2023

FiNGERPRINT! CLASSICS
An imprint of Prakash Books India Pvt. Ltd

113/A, Darya Ganj,
New Delhi-110 002
Email: info@prakashbooks.com/sales@prakashbooks.com

facebook www.facebook.com/fingerprintpublishing
twitter www.twitter.com/FingerprintP
www.fingerprintpublishing.com

ISBN: 978 93 5856 172 2

Processed & printed in India

Ernst Theodor Wilhelm Hoffmann, also known as E.T.A. Hoffmann, was a German writer, composer, and artist of the Romantic era. Born on January 24, 1776, in Königsberg, Prussia (now Kaliningrad, Russia), Hoffmann was a prolific author of short stories, novels, and music criticism, as well as a composer of operas and other musical works.

Hoffmann's literary career began with his legal profession, but his passion for art and literature led him to abandon law and pursue creative endeavors. His writing is known for its dark, fantastical themes and exploration of the human psyche. His most famous works include *Nutcracker and Mouse King*, which served as the basis for the ballet *The Nutcracker,* and *The Sandman*—a story about a man who is haunted by a childhood trauma.

Written in 1816, *Nutcracker and Mouse King* tells the story of a young girl named Marie, who receives a nutcracker doll as a Christmas gift and goes on a magical adventure with him. The story has been adapted into numerous stage productions, films, and ballets.

In addition to his writing, Hoffmann was a talented musician and composer. He studied music at the University of Königsberg and later became a music director in various cities all over Germany. He also wrote music criticism for several publications, including the influential *Allgemeine musikalische Zeitung*.

Hoffmann's work had a significant influence on the Romantic movement in literature and music. His writing style inspired writers such as Edgar Allan Poe and Nathaniel Hawthorne, and his music criticism helped the development of German Romantic music.

Despite his success as a writer and musician, Hoffmann faced numerous personal and professional struggles throughout his life. One significant challenge was his battle with his mental health issues, such as depression, anxiety, and paranoia. These struggles often found their way into his works, infusing them with darkness and psychological turmoil. Additionally, his career as a lawyer was marked by setbacks and frustrations, and he faced financial difficulties for much of his life. Despite his passion for the arts, he struggled to gain recognition and support for his creative endeavors, which often left him feeling marginalized and underappreciated. He died in Berlin in 1822, at the age of 46.

Today, Hoffmann is remembered as a master of the Romantic literary and musical traditions. His stories continue to captivate readers with their vivid imagery and psychological depth, and his music remains an important part of the German Romantic repertoire.

CONTENTS

1.	Christmas Eve	7
2.	The Gifts	13
3.	The Protégé	19
4.	Marvels	25
5.	The Battle	35
6.	The Illness	41
7.	The Tale of the Hard Nut	47
8.	Continuation of the Tale of the Hard Nut	55
9.	Conclusion of the Tale of the Hard Nut	61

10.	Uncle and Nephew	71
11.	Victory	75
12.	The Kingdom of Dolls	85
13.	The Capital	91
14.	Conclusion	101

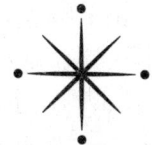

CHRISTMAS EVE

For the entire twenty-fourth of December, the children of Medical Officer Stahlbaum were not permitted to step inside the intermediary room, much less the magnificent showcase next door. Fritz and Marie sat huddled together in a corner of the back room. The deep evening dusk had set in, and the children felt quite eerie because, as was usual on this day, no light had been brought in. Fritz quite secretly whispered to his younger sister (she had just turned seven) that he had heard a rustling and murmuring and soft throbbing in the locked rooms since early that morning. Also, not so long ago (Fritz went on), a short, dark man with a large casket under his arm had stolen across the vestibule. However, said Fritz, he knew quite well that it was none other than Godfather Drosselmeier.

Marie joyfully clapped her little hands and exclaimed: "Ah, I wonder what lovely presents he's made for us!"

Supreme Court Justice Drosselmeier was anything but handsome. He was short and scrawny, his face was covered with wrinkles, and he wore a big, black patch instead of a right eye. He also had no hair on his head, which is why he sported a very lovely periwig made of spun glass and very artistic. Indeed, the godfather was altogether a very artistic man, who even knew a thing or two about clocks and could actually build them. So if any of the beautiful clocks in Stahlbaum's home fell ill and couldn't sing, Godfather Drosselmeier would come by, remove his glass periwig, take off his snug yellow vest, tie on a blue apron, and insert sharp instruments into the gears. It was very painful for little Marie, but it didn't harm the clock at all. In fact, the clock even grew lively, and it started cheerfully humming, striking, and singing again, much to everyone's delight.

Whenever Drosselmeier visited them, he would bring something nice for the children. His pocket might contain a manikin that could twist its eyes and bow—which was comical to see. Or Drosselmeier might have a box from which a little bird came hopping out, or he might have something utterly different. But for Christmas, Drosselmeier always completed a gorgeous artistic work, which cost him a great effort. That is why, after showing the gift, the parents very cautiously stored it away.

"Ah, I wonder what lovely presents he's made for us," Marie exclaimed.

Fritz decided that this year it could be nothing but a fortress, where all kinds of very handsome soldiers drilled and marched to and fro. Next, other soldiers would have to storm and invade the fortress. But now the inside soldiers boldly shot their cannons, making them boom and burst.

"No, no!" Marie interrupted Fritz. "Godfather Drosselmeier told me about a beautiful park with a huge lake and with marvelous swans gliding about and wearing gold neckbands and singing the loveliest songs. Then a little girl comes to the lake and entices the swans and feeds them sweet marzipan."

"Swans don't eat marzipan," Fritz broke in quite roughly, "and Godfather Drosselmeier can't make a whole park. Actually, we get little out of his toys. They're promptly taken away from us. So I much prefer what Mama and Papa give us. We can keep their presents nicely and do whatever we like with them."

Now the children debated what their parents would bring them. Marie felt that Fräulein Trutchen (her large doll) was changing deeply. For, clumsier than ever, she fell on the floor every moment. This didn't happen without a nasty grin, and there was no further thought of the cleanliness of her garments.

Nor did a thorough scolding help. Also, Mama, we are told, smiled with such delight at Gretchen's small parasol. Fritz, by contrast, assured the others that his royal stable lacked a good sorrel, just as his troops fully lacked a cavalry—Papa was well aware of that.

So the children knew that their parents had bought them all kinds of beautiful presents, which they now displayed. But the children were also certain that the dear Holy Christ shone upon them with the pious and friendly eyes of children. And they were equally convinced that, as if touched by fruitful hands, every Christmas gift would bring marvelous pleasure like no other.

The children, who kept whispering about the expected presents, were reminded of that pleasure by their older sister, Luise. And they added that it was now also the Holy Christ, who, through the hands of their dear parents, always gave them whatever real joy and pleasure He could bring them. Indeed, He knew that a lot better than did the children themselves, who didn't have to nurture all sorts of hopes and wishes. Rather, they had to wait, still and pious, for their Christmas presents.

Little Marie grew pensive, while Fritz murmured to himself: "I'd love to have a sorrel and Hussars."

By now it had grown completely dark. Fritz and Marie, thoroughly pressed together, did not dare say another word. It sounded as if rustling wings encircled them, and as if they could catch a very distant and very splendid music. A bright shine grazed the wall, and now the children knew that the Christ Child had flown away on radiant clouds, flown to other happy children.

At that moment, they heard a bright silvery chime: "Klingling, klingling!"

The doors burst open, and the radiance erupting into the large room was so deep that the children cried out: "Ah! Ah!" and they halted on the threshold, petrified.

But then Mama and Papa stepped in, took the children by the hand, and said: "Come on, come on, you dear children, and look what the Holy Christ has brought you."

THE GIFTS

I turn to you, gentle reader or listener—Fritz, Theodor, Emst—or whatever your name may be, and I picture you vividly at your last Christmas table, which is richly adorned with gorgeous, multicolored presents. You will then envisage how the children halted, in silence and with shining eyes. You will then envision how, after a while, Marie cried out with a deep sigh: "Ah! How beautiful! Ah! How beautiful!" And Fritz tried out his caprioles, which were very successful. But the children had to have been devout and well behaved the entire year, for never had they had such splendid and such beautiful gifts as this time.

The huge fir tree in the center carried many gold and silver apples, and, like buds and blossoms, the sugared almonds and colorful bonbons and goodness knows what other tidbits emerged from all the branches. However, the loveliest and most praiseworthy feature of the wonder tree was the myriad of tiny lights that twinkled like tiny stars in its dark boughs. And the tree itself, shining in and out, warmly invited the children to pick its blooms and fruits. Around the tree, everything shone very grand and bright—what gorgeous things there were—why, who could describe them all?

Marie saw the most delicate dolls, all kinds of small, clean implements, and, what was loveliest to view: a silk frock, daintily garnished with parti-colored ribbons, hung from a rack right in front of Marie, so she could observe the dress from all sides. And that is what she did, while exclaiming over and over: "Oh, the darling little frock, oh, the lovely little frock! And I'll be quite confident that I'll be allowed to wear it!"

Meanwhile, Fritz, trotting and galloping around the table three or four times, was testing the new sorrel, which he had indeed found on the table, fenced in. Climbing back down, Fritz thought that the sorrel was a wild beast. But it didn't matter, Fritz would certainly overcome it. And he mustered the new squadrons of Hussars, who were magnificently garbed in red and gold and carried silver weapons. The horses they were riding were so shiny white you might have almost believed that they were pure silver too.

The children, a bit calmer now, wanted to pounce on the picture books, which were lying open, so you could see all sorts of very lovely blossoms and gaudy people and delightful children playing. And they were all painted so naturally as if they could truly live and speak.

Yes, indeed. The children were about to pounce on these wonderful books when the doorbell rang again. Knowing that now Godfather Drosselmeier would offer his gifts, the children ran over to the table, which was standing alongside the wall. The screen that had hidden the table for such a long time was quickly removed. And what did the children witness?!

On a green lawn embellished with colorful flowers stood a fabulous castle with many plate-glass windows and golden turrets. A glockenspiel resounded, doors and windows opened, and you could see very tiny but dainty ladies and gentlemen in plumed hats and with long trains strolling through the chambers. The middle room had so many burning candles in silver chandeliers that it looked as if it were fully ablaze, and children in short vests and jerkins were dancing to the sound of the glockenspiel. A gentleman in an emerald cape often peered through the window, beckoned to the onlookers, and disappeared again—just as Godfather Drosselmeier himself, but scarcely larger than Papa's thumb, at times stood below, at the castle gates, then stepped back inside.

With elbows propped on the table, Fritz had looked at the beautiful castle and the strolling and dancing figurines. Then he said: "Godfather Drosselmeier! Let me into your castle!"

Drosselmeier indicated that this was out of the question. And he was right. For it was foolish of Fritz to wish to enter a castle that, together with its golden turrets, was not as tall as Fritz himself.

And Fritz understood.

After a time—when the ladies and gentlemen were strolling to and fro in the same fashion, the children were dancing, the emerald man was peering out the same window, and Godfather Drosselmeier stationed himself at the gates—Fritz asked impatiently: "Godfather Drosselmeier, why don't you come out through the other door over there?!"

"That won't do, dear little Fritz," Drosselmeier replied.

"Well, then let him go," Fritz went on. "Let the green man go strolling with the others. After all, he keeps peering out."

"That won't do either," Drosselmeier again replied.

"Then tell the children to come down," cried Fritz. "I want to investigate them more closely."

"Oh, none of this will really do," said Drosselmeier, annoyed. "The mechanics are set up, and that's how they must stay."

"Reeaaaly?" Fritz drawled. "None of this will do? Listen, Godfather Drosselmeier. If those small polished things in the castle can only keep repeating themselves, then they're not worth much, and I don't especially have to call for them. I need to praise my Hussars. They have to maneuver forward, backward—whatever I wish, and they're not locked in any house."

And with that, Fritz jumped out toward the Christmas table, and he had his squadron leap back and forth on his silver horses, trotting and wheeling and smashing and firing to his heart's content.

Marie had likewise stolen away so gently, for she too had soon gotten fed up with the dancing and meandering of the tiny dolls in the castle; though, well behaved and well brought up as she was, she didn't voice her annoyances did Brother Fritz.

Drosselmeier spoke rather crossly to the parents: "Such artistic work is not meant for senseless children. I'm simply going to pack up my castle!"

However, the mother came over and had the godfather explain the inner construction and the very wonderful and very creative gear unit, which set teensy dolls moving. The counselor took everything apart and then put it together again. While laboring, he turned cheerful again, and he gave the children a few lovely tan men and women with golden hands, legs, and faces. They were made entirely out of the fanciest gingerbread and they were so sweet and pleasant as to greatly delight Fritz and Marie.

Sister Luise, as Mother wished, had put on the lovely frock that was one of her gifts, and she looked gorgeous. However, when she was likewise about to don her dress, Marie felt that she would rather see it on Luise for a bit. And her mother was glad to comply..

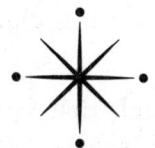

THE PROTÉGÉ

Actually, Marie didn't want to leave the Christmas table, for she had discovered something that no one else had as yet noticed. You see, the review of Fritz's Hussars, who had paraded closely past the tree, had revealed an excellent little man, who stood there, quiet and modest, as if calmly awaiting his turn. Granted, there was a lot to object to in his stature; for aside from the fact that his somewhat lengthy and powerful upper body didn't quite fit in with the tiny, skinny legs, his head likewise seemed much too big.

To a great extent, amends were made by his attractive clothes, which suggested a man of taste and breeding. After all, he sported a very lovely, shiny, violet dolman with countless white braids and buttons. He also wore the loveliest trousers and finest ankle boots that had ever graced the feet of a student, much less an officer. These boots were as snug on the delicate little legs as if they were a perfect fit. Now it was funny that he had donned a miner's cap and that he had accompanied his garb in back with a slim, clumsy cape that looked like wood.

Meanwhile, Marie felt that Godfather Drosselmeier had also slung an awful morning coat around his shoulders and put on a dreadful cap—but he was still a very dear godfather. Marie had likewise mused that no matter how delicate the little man, the godfather would never be as appealing as he. The little girl had instantly liked the nice man, and the more she looked at him, the more she realized what a gentle and kindly face he had. The light green, bulging eyes promised nothing but friendship and benevolence. It was good for the man to place a well-groomed, white-cotton beard on his chin, since you could perceive the sweet smile of the deep red lips all the more clearly.

"Ah!" Marie finally exclaimed. "Ah! Dear Father! Who owns that darling little man over on the tree there?"

"He," the father answered. "He, dear child, should work hard for all of us. He should crack the hard nuts for us nicely. And he should belong to Luise as much as he belongs to you and to Fritz."

The father then removed him cautiously from the table and, raising the wooden cape aloft, the manikin opened his mouth wide, wide, and showed two rows of very sharp, very tiny white teeth. When told to do so, Marie inserted a nut and—Crack! Crack!—he chewed up the nut, so that the shell dropped away, and the sweet kernel itself ended up in Marie's hand.

By now, everyone, including Marie, had to know that the dainty little man was an offspring of the dynasty of Nutcrackers and was practicing his profession.

She shouted for joy, but then her father spoke:

"Since, dear Marie, you love Friend Nutcracker so much, you must shield and shelter him especially, even despite the fact that, as I have said, Luise and Fritz have as much right to use him as you!"

Marie promptly took Nutcracker in her arms and had him crack nuts, though she picked the smallest ones. That way the manikin wouldn't have to open his mouth very wide, which basically didn't look so good. Luise joined Marie, and Friend Nutcracker also had to perform his duties for Luise—which he didn't seem to mind doing, since he smiled very amiably all the time.

Fritz, meanwhile, had grown tired from all the riding and drilling, and when he heard the pleasurable cracking of nuts, he sprang over to his sisters and roared with laughter at the quaint manikin. Now that Fritz also wanted to eat nuts, the little man passed from hand to hand, unable to halt his snapping open and shut. Fritz kept shoving in the biggest and hardest nuts. All at once, they heard a double crack. Then three little teeth fell out of Nutcracker's mouth, and his whole lower jaw turned loose and wobbly.

"Oh, my poor, dear Nutcracker," Marie exclaimed, whisking him out of Fritz's hands.

"He's a stupid, simpleminded guy!" said Fritz. "He wants to be a Nutcracker, but he has no decent teeth. He probably doesn't understand his own work. Hand him over, Marie! He has to chew up nuts for me, even if he loses his remaining teeth—even his entire jaw in the bargain. Who cares about that good-for-nothing?!"

"No! No!" Marie wept. "You're not going to get him—my dear Nutcracker! Just look at the way he watches me so sorrowfully and shows me his little, injured mouth! But you're a coldhearted person, Fritz—you beat your horses and you even let a soldier be shot dead!"

"That's the way it has to be, you just don't understand," cried Fritz. "Anyway, Nutcracker belongs to me as much as he belongs to you! Hand him over!!"

Marie began sobbing hard and she quickly wrapped up the sick Nutcracker in her tiny handkerchief. The parents came over with Godfather Drosselmeier, who, to Marie's great regret, sided with Fritz.

However, her father said: "I deliberately placed Nutcracker under Marie's protection. And now that I see she needs him, she has full power over Nutcracker with no interference from anyone. Incidentally, I'm very surprised that Fritz demands further services from somebody who has been injured in service. After all, as a good military man, he should know that wounded soldiers never line up in rank and file."

Fritz was very ashamed and, without concerning himself any further about nuts and about Nutcracker, he stole over to the other side of the table. There, after setting the appropriate outposts, the Hussars had gone to their night quarters.

As for Marie, she hunted down Nutcracker's little lost teeth. Around his wounded chin, she had wrapped a lovely white ribbon, which she had detached from her frock and bound up. The poor little man had looked very pale and frightened, and so Marie had wrapped him more gingerly than before in her cloth. Cradling him in her arms like a baby, she looked at the lovely pictures in the new picture book, which lay out today among all the other gifts.

Contrary to her usual behavior, Marie got quite angry when Godfather Drosselmeier kept laughing and asking how she managed to remain so lovely despite that thoroughly hideous manikin. Now she recalled the bizarre comparison she had drawn with Drosselmeier at first sight, and she spoke very earnestly:

"Who knows, dear Godfather, if you were spruced up like my dear Nutcracker, and if you had on such lovely, shiny ankle boots, who knows if you wouldn't be as beautiful as he?"

Marie couldn't tell why her parents laughed so loudly and why Supreme Court Counselor developed a red nose and didn't laugh as clearly as before. There must have been a special reason.

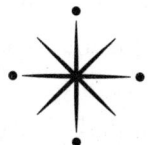

MARVELS

When you step through the door, into the home of the medical counselor, you'll find a tall glass cabinet on the broad wall to your left. The shelves store all the lovely presents that are given to the children every year. Luise was still very little when her father ordered the cabinet from a very skillful cabinetmaker. The man inserted the panes so brightly—indeed, he knew how to equip the entire showcase so adroitly that everything inside looked almost shinier and lovelier than if you were holding it yourself.

The top shelf, unattainable for Marie and Fritz, held Drosselmeier's artworks. Right below was the shelf for the picture books. The two lowest shelves could be filled by Marie and Fritz, however they wished. But usually, Marie assigned the bottom shelf for her dolls to live on, while, on the shelf overhead, Fritz drove his troops into the cantonments.

The same thing had happened today. While Fritz had stationed his Hussars overhead, Marie had put Fräulein Trutchen aside, had placed the new and spruced-up doll in the very elegantly appointed room, and had invited herself to some delicious confectionary with Marie.

The room was appointed very elegantly—so I've said, and it's also true.

For I don't know if you, my attentive reader Marie, like little Miss Stahlbaum (you already know that she too is called Marie), ah! I wonder if the little girl has a small, lovely, flowery sofa like this Marie. Do they have several darling little chairs, a dainty tea table—and above all, a little spic-and-span bed, where the prettiest dolls rest?

All these things were in the corner of the cabinet, whose walls were papered here with little parti-colored pictures. And you can imagine that the new doll, who, as Marie learned that same evening, was named Fräulein Clärchen, had to feel very wonderful in this room.

It was late evening—indeed, midnight was approaching, and Drosselmeier had long since gone home. However, Marie and Fritz still couldn't leave the glass cabinet, no matter how much their mother kept ordering them to finally get to bed.

"It's true!" Fritz exclaimed at last. "Those poor guys!" (He meant his Hussars!) "They want to have their rest too. And so long as I'm here, no one dares to catch forty winks—I already know that!"

Fritz left, but Marie begged and begged: "Just a wee bit longer—please, dear Mother, let me stay just a wee bit longer. I have to take care of a few things. When I'm done, I'll go straight to bed!"

Marie was a devout and reasonable child, and so her good mother had no qualms about leaving her alone with her toys.

Still, her mother wanted to keep Marie from being all too deeply tempted by the new doll and the lovely playthings. Forgetting about the candles burning all around the wall closet, the mother snuffed all of them, so that only the lamp suspended in the middle of the ceiling spread a gentle, graceful light.

"Come in soon, dear Marie! Otherwise you won't get up at the right time tomorrow!" exclaimed the mother, withdrawing into the bedroom.

As soon as Marie was alone, she quickly went over to do what was quite properly on her mind and what she could not tell her mother, though she did not know why. Marie still had the wounded Nutcracker wrapped in her handkerchief, and she carried him in her arms.

Now she placed him cautiously on the table, unwrapped him softly, softly, and tended to the injuries.

Nutcracker was very pale, but he beamed so ruefully and amiably that his smile shot right through her heart.

"Ah, dear little Nutcracker," she murmured very softly. "Please don't be angry at me because my brother Fritz hurt you so deeply. He didn't really mean it so badly. He's just gotten a bit hard-hearted in the wild military. Otherwise, he's a truly fine boy—you can count on it.

"But now I want to nurse you very tenderly until you're fully sound and cheery again. As for reinserting your little teeth thoroughly and properly and straightening out your shoulders, Godfather Drosselmeier can take care of all that—he's an expert in such matters."

However, Marie could not finish. For when she pronounced Drosselmeier's name, Friend Nutcracker's face twisted up devilishly, and his eyes virtually emitted sparkling green prickles. But the moment Marie tried to get properly released, she was again viewed by the mournfully smiling face of honest Nutcracker. And now she knew that it was the draft and the quickly blazing ray of the lamp that had totally distorted his features.

"Aren't I a silly little girl—scared so easily that I even believe this little wooden doll can make faces? Still, I care so much for Nutcracker because he's so funny, and yet so kind, and that's why he has to be nursed as is proper!"

Marie now took Friend Nutcracker by the arm, went over to the glass cabinet, huddled in front of it, and spoke to the new doll: "Please, pretty please, Fräulein Clärchen, please give up my little bed for sick, wounded Nutcracker, and make do with the sofa as best you can. Don't forget that you're very healthy and powerful. Otherwise, you wouldn't have such thick dark red cheeks. And don't forget that very few of the most gorgeous dolls own such soft couches."

In her full, shiny Christmas garb, Fräulein Clärchen looked very noble and very angry, and she didn't breathe a word.

"Now, why am I making such a fuss?" said Marie.

She pulled out the bed, tucked dear Nutcracker in very gently and delicately, and wrapped him up with a beautiful little ribbon. She normally rapped the ribbon around her body; however, this time, she wrapped it around his injured shoulders and covered him all the way up to her nose.

"But he mustn't remain with naughty Clärchen," Marie went on. She pulled up the little bed together with Nutcracker (who was lying on it) and she placed them on the top shelf. In this way, the little bed lay right next to the lovely village where Fritz's Hussars were billeted.

Marie locked the cabinet and was about to go into the bedroom, when—now listen, children!—when she caught a soft, soft whispering and murmuring and rustling all around, behind the oven, behind the chairs, behind the cabinets. The wall clock hummed louder and louder, but it couldn't strike.

Marie looked up. The big, gilded owl perching on the clock had lowered its wings, covering the whole timepiece and poking forth the ugly cobblestone with the hooked nose. And the noises grew louder, and words could be made out: "Clock, tick, tock, clock, tick, tock!

And everyone has to hum softly, hum softly. After all, Mouse King has a fine ear.

"Hummmmm, hummmmmm, hummmmmm. Strike, chime, do/Soon there will be few!"

And the humming resounded dull and hoarse twelve times!

Marie shuddered dreadfully and she would almost have dashed off in horror if she had not spotted Godfather Drosselmeier, who sat on the wall clock in lieu of the owl, his yellow coattails dangling like wings on both sides.

However, Marie pulled herself together and she exclaimed, loudly and tearfully:

"Godfather Drosselmeier, Godfather Drosselmeier, what are you doing up there? Come down to me and stop frightening me, you nasty Godfather Drosselmeier!"

However, now a wild giggling and whistling started all around and virtually a thousand little feet were trotting and scurrying behind the walls and virtually a thousand little candle stubs were flickering through the cracks in the floorboards. Still these weren't candle stubs, no! These were tiny, sparkling eyes. And Marie realized that mice were peering out and preparing themselves everywhere.

Soon the room reverberated with trot, trot, and hop, hop, brighter and denser squads of mice were galloping to and fro and they finally lined up in rank and file, the way Fritz stationed his soldiers before a battle.

Marie found this very funny, and, unlike some other children, she didn't have a natural aversion to mice. Indeed, she was about to shed any terror she might have felt, when all at once the room began to whistle so sharply and so outrageously that she had to shudder! Ah, what did she notice now?

No, truly, my honored reader Fritz, I know that your heart is in the right place, just like the heart of the wise and bold General Fritz Stahlbaum. But if you had seen what Marie now saw, you would have truly dashed away. I even feel that you would have leaped into bed and pulled the cover much farther over your ears than necessary.

Ah! Poor Marie could not do even that. For just listen, children. Right at her feet, as if driven by subterranean force, the ground spurted out sand and lime and crumbling wall stones, and seven mouse heads with seven brightly sparkling crowns loomed high from the ground, hissing and whistling quite unbearably.

Soon the mouse body, to whose neck the seven heads were attached, likewise worked its way out completely, and the large mouse, adorned with seven diadems, exulted in its full chorus. Squeaking loudly three times, the mouse faced the entire army, which suddenly got moving. Hott, hott, trott, trott, it headed straight toward the cabinet, ah, straight toward Marie, who was standing right up against the glass door.

Marie's heart had beaten so loudly in fear and terror that she thought it might burst out of her chest, and she would then have to die. But now she felt as if the blood were frozen in her veins. Half fainting, she staggered backward, hearing klirr, klirr, purr, purr, and the glass pane of the cabinet, elbowed by Marie, collapsed in fragments.

At that moment, Marie did feel a truly sharp pain in her left arm, but her heart suddenly felt much lighter. She now heard no squeaking or piping; everything was very still. And even though she didn't care to have a look, she did believe that the mice, frightened by the tinkling of the glass shards, had retreated to their own holes.

But just what was that?

Right behind Marie, strange noises were now heard from the cabinet, and very fine voices resounded: "Wake up, wake up, to the battle this very night! Wake up, wake up to the battle!" And harmonious chimes jingled sweetly and gracefully.

"Ah! That's my little glockenspiel," cried Marie, jumping aside.

Now she saw a bizarre lighting in the cabinet, a puttering and fiddling around. There were several dolls, hurrying and scurrying about, and fighting with their skinny arms.

All at once, Nutcracker sat up, flung the cover far away, and leaped out of bed with both feet, shouting: "Crack, crack, crack! Foolish mice pack! Crick, crack, real sack!" And with that, Nutcracker drew his little sword and waved it in the air and cried: "You, my dear friends and vassals and brothers, do you wish to help me in the hard struggle?"

Three Scaramouches promptly retorted, as did one Pantaloon, four chimney sweeps, two zitherists, and one drummer: "Yessir, we submit to you in steadfast devotion, and we march with you into death, struggle, and victory!"

And they followed the passionate Nutcracker, who dared to make the perilous leap from the top shelf. It was no use their jumping. For not only did they wear rich garments of cloth and silk, but there wasn't much more inside them than chaff and cotton. That was why they plopped down like sacks of wool.

Poor Nutcracker would certainly have broken his arms and his legs. For—just imagine—it was nearly two feet high above the shelf where he was standing until the bottom, and his body was as brittle as if carved out of linden wood. Yes indeed! Nutcracker would have certainly broken his arms and his legs if, in the moment of his leap, Fräulein Clärchen had not also jumped from the sofa and caught the hero's drawn sword in her soft arms.

"Ah, you dear, sweet Clärchen!" Marie sobbed. "How I misunderstood you! You would have certainly been glad to give up your little bed to Friend Nutcracker!"

But now Fräulein Clärchen spoke, pressing the young hero gently against her silken breast: "If you do not wish, oh lord, sick and wounded as you are, to join the struggle and the peril, then see how your courageous vassals, belligerent and certain of victory, gather together. Scaramouch, Pantaloon, Chimney Sweep, Zitherist, and Drummer are already downstairs. And the coat-of-arms figures on my shelf actually throb and thump noticeably! You may wish, sir, to rest in my arms or watch your victory from my plumed hat!"

Those were Clärchen's words. But Nutcracker was so very unruly and he kicked so hard that Clärchen had to drop him on the floor. However, at that instant, Nutcracker knelt down politely on one knee and whispered:

"Oh, my lady, I will remember you in charm and grace while I tussle and struggle!"

Clärchen bent down so deep that she was able to clutch Nutcracker's skinny arm, and she gently pulled him up. Then she quickly detached herself with her multispangled girdle and she was about to hang it around Fritz's neck. But Fritz stepped back two paces, put his hand on his chest, and spoke very solemnly:

"Do not, oh my lady, wish to waste your grace on me." He faltered, took a deep breath, and then he tore the ribbon from Marie's shoulders—he pressed the ribbon against his lips. Fritz now hung the ribbon around his waist like an officer's sash. And then, boldly swinging his naked sword, quickly and nimbly, he sprang like a tiny bird across the ridge on the floor. You must notice, very gentle and excellent readers, that when Nutcracker had come alive, he had quite clearly felt all the love and kindness that Marie had shown him. It was only because she had become so good that Fritz did not even want to accept and wear Fräulein's ribbon, although it shone brightly and looked very lovely. Good, loyal Nutcracker preferred getting all spruced up with Marie's simple little ribbon.

Now what comes next?

When Nutcracker springs down, the squealing and squeaking likewise resume.

Ah! The obnoxious crews of countless mice stay under the big table, and the horrible mouse with the seven heads looms over all of them!

What is next?!

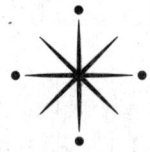

THE BATTLE

"Beat to the general march, my loyal vassal, Drummer!" Nutcracker yelled. Drummer instantly rolled the drum so artistically that the panes of the glass cabinet shivered and shuddered. The interior cracked and clabbered, and Marie realized something about the covers of all the boxes in which Fritz's army was billeted. The covers violently jumped up, and the soldiers leaped out and down in the bottom shelf, where they collected in glossy teams.

Nutcracker scurried to and fro, speaking enthusiastic words to the troops: "No dog of a trumpeter stirs and shifts!" Nutcracker shrieked angrily. Then he quickly turned to Pantaloon, who grew somewhat pale, his nose wobbling and wobbling. Nutcracker spoke solemnly:

"General, I am well aware of your courage and your experience. The goals here are a rapid survey and a use of the moment. I entrust you with the command of all the cavalries and artilleries. You don't need a horse; you've got very long legs and you can gallop quite decently. Now carry out your vocation."

Pantaloon immediately squeezed his long, dry fingers against his mouth, and he crowed so piercingly that it sounded like a hundred bright trumpets blowing cheerfully away. A neighing and stamping now emerged in the cabinet, and lo and behold: Fritz's cuirassiers and dragoons and especially the shiny new Hussars marched out and soon halted down below on the floor.

Now regiment upon regiment defiled past Nutcracker with flying colors and fife and drum and presented itself in rank and file across the floor of the room. However, Fritz's cannons then rolled up, clanking, and surrounded by the cannoneers, and soon the cannons went boom—boom, and Marie saw the sugar peas smash into the thick pile of mice that were covered with white powder and were very ashamed. Above all, however, they suffered great damage by a heavy battery, which had rolled up on Mama's footstool, and boom—boom—boom and shot gingerbreads in succession and under the mice, which made them drop.

But then the mice came nearer and nearer and they even over-ran a few cannons; which sounded—prr—prr—prr, and in the smoke and dust, Marie could scarcely see what was happening. Yet so much was certain: Every corps fought with supreme vehemence, and for a long time victory swung back and forth. The mice kept developing more and more masses; and their tiny silvery pills, which they hurled very cleverly, were now striking the interior of the glass cabinet. Clärchen and Trutchen desperately scurried about, wringing their little hands sore.

"Should I die in the flower of my youth?! I, the loveliest of the dolls?!" cried Clärchen.

"Have I preserved myself so well as to perish here inside my four walls?" cried Trutchen.

They flung their arms around each other and they bawled so dreadfully that you could hear them despite the huge racket. For, gentle reader, you barely have an inkling of the uproar that now began:

Prr—prr—pudd—pidd—taratantara—taratantara—boom—boom—boom—all tangled up!

And Mouse King and mice squealed and shrieked, and they again heard Nutcracker's tremendous voice issuing useful orders, and they watched Nutcracker as he marched over the battalions standing in the line of fire. Pantaloon launched a few brilliant cavalry attacks and covered himself with glory.

But Fritz's Hussars were pelted by the mouse artillery with ugly, smelly bullets, which left nasty stains on their red jerkins—and that is why they didn't care to go ahead.

Furthermore, Pantaloon ordered them to wheel to the left. And in the enthusiasm of commanding, he did likewise, and so did his dragoons and cuirassiers—that is, they all wheeled to the left and went home. In so doing, the battery perching on the footstool was endangered. And it wasn't very long before a dense squad of very hideous mice charged so heavily that the entire footstool toppled over together with cannons and cannoneers. Nutcracker, who seemed very dazed, ordered the right wing to retreat. You know—oh my experienced listener Fritz—that a retreat is almost the same as a flight. And you already join me in mourning because of the misfortune that afflicted the army of little Marie as loved by Nutcracker!

But avert your eyes from this disaster and view the left wing of Nutcracker's army, where everything is still good, and much is to be expected from the general and the army. During the most heated fighting, quiet, quiet masses of mouse cavaliers had come debouching out from under the dresser and, amid noisy, gruesome squealing, they had thrown themselves on the left wing of Nutcracker's army—but what resistance they encountered! Slowly, as the difficulties of the terrain allowed, they had to pass the ridge of the cabinet. The corps bearing the coat of arms had advanced under the leadership of two Chinese emperors, and had formed itself en carré plaine.

The Battle

These brave, splendid, and colorful troops, which consisted of many gardeners, Tyroleans, Tunguses, barbers, Harlequins, cupids, lions, tigers, apes, and long-tailed monkeys, fought with great courage, deep composure, and tough endurance. This battalion of elitists, showing Spartan boldness, would have torn victory from the foe, if a daring enemy horse captain had not recklessly plunged forward and bitten off the head of one Chinese emperor, who, in falling, would have then killed two Tunguses and a long-tailed monkey. The result was a hole through which the enemy pushed in, and soon the entire battalion was chewed up. However, the enemy had little profit from this atrocity. Just as a bloodthirsty mouse cavalierist chewed up a bold opponent straight to the middle, the mouse was given a small printed slip of paper down his throat, from which he promptly died. But did this help Nutcracker's army, which, having begun its retreat, now drew farther and farther, losing more and more men, so that unfortunate Nutcracker was left with just a tiny squad right in front of the glass cabinet?

"The reserves step forward! Pantaloon, Scaramouch, Drummer—where are you?" Nutcracker was hollering, hoping for fresh troops, which were to be deployed out of the glass cabinet. Indeed, a few brown men and women actually emerged with gingerbreads, golden faces, hats and helmets in advance. But they fought so clumsily that they struck none of the enemies; and soon they would have even knocked Commander Nutcracker's cap off his head.

The enemy chasseurs also bit off their legs, so that they toppled over, killing a few of Nutcracker's comrades-in-arms. Nutcracker was now densely surrounded by the enemy, in the highest fear and distress. He wanted to jump across the cabinet ridge, but his legs were too short. Clärchen and Trutchen lay there unconscious—they couldn't help. Hussars and dragoons sprang merrily past him and into the fray! He now yelled in utter despair: "A horse, a horse, my kingdom for a horse!"

At that instant, two enemy tirailleurs grabbed him by his wooden cape and, triumphantly squealing out of seven throats, Mouse King came leaping up. Marie could no longer contain herself. "Oh, my poor Nutcracker! My poor Nutcracker!" she sobbed, snatching her left shoe and, not quite aware of what she was doing, she flung her shoe into the thickest squad of mice—at their king! At that moment, everything seemed to fade and waft away. But Marie felt an even sharper pain in her left arm—sharper than before—and she fainted dead to the world.

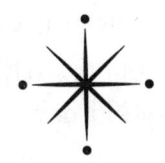

THE ILLNESS

When Marie awoke as if from a deathly coma, she found herself in her little bed. The sun shone, twinkling and sparkling through the icy windows into the room. Right next to Marie sat a stranger, whom she soon recognized as the surgeon Dr. Wendelstern. He murmured softly: "She's awake."

Now her mother came over and scrutinized her anxiously. "Ah, dear Mother," whispered little Marie, "are all the ugly mice now gone, and is good Nutcracker saved?"

"Don't talk such nonsense, dear Marie!" her mother replied. "What do the mice have to do with Nutcracker? But you, you naughty child. You've caused us so much worry and anguish. That's what happens when children are willful and disobey their parents. Yesterday, you played with your dolls until late at night. You grew drowsy, and perhaps you were startled by a protruding mouse, which is usually not found in this area. In any case, you shoved your arm into a pane in the glass cabinet. The cut was so deep that Dr. Wendelstern, who removed the glass fragments from the wounds, felt that if the glass had sliced an artery, you would have retained a stiff arm or even bled to death.

"Thank goodness that when I awoke at midnight and missed you so late, I got up and stepped into the living room. You were lying unconscious on the floor right next to the glass cabinet, bleeding torrents. I was so scared that I nearly blacked out myself. There you lay, and scattered all round you were many of Fritz's lead soldiers and other dolls, shattered coats of arms and gingerbread men. Nutcracker, however, lay on your bleeding arm, and not far from here lay your left shoe."

"Oh, Mama! Mama darling!" Marie broke in. "Just look! Those were the traces of the great clash between the dolls and the mice. And that's why I was startled—when the mice wanted to capture poor Nutcracker, who was in command of the army of dolls. I hurled my shoe at the mice, but I don't know what happened next."

The Illness

Dr. Wendelstern winked at the mother, who spoke very gently to Marie: "Let it be, my dear child! Calm down, the mice are all gone, and Nutcracker is standing in the glass cabinet, healthy and cheery."

Now the medical officer came into the room and he had a long talk with Dr. Wendelstern. Next the medical officer felt Marie's pulse. And she heard something about a wound fever. Marie had to stay in bed and take medicine. And she did so for several days, even though she didn't feel sick or uneasy aside from some pains in her arm. She knew that Nutcracker had escaped the battle safe and sound, and at times she felt as if she were dreaming that he spoke to her quite lucidly though mournfully:

"Marie, dearest lady, I already owe you a great deal. But you can do even more for me."

She pondered and pondered, but it was no use, she couldn't figure out what Nutcracker meant.

The girl couldn't play at all because of her injured arm. And if she wanted to read or to leaf through one of the picture books, her head swam, and she was forced to stop looking.

Time must now have been inching along very slowly, and Marie could hardly wait until twilight, when Mother would sit at her bedside and read a lot to her or tell her lovely stories. Mother had just finished the wonderful tale of Prince Fakardin, when the door opened, and Godfather Drosselmeier walked in, saying: "Now I really have to see the sick and wounded girl for myself."

The instant Marie spotted Godfather Drosselmeier in his yellow jacket, she so vividly recalled the night when Nutcracker lost the battle with the mice. Now she involuntarily exclaimed to her godfather:

"Oh, Godfather Drosselmeier, you were quite ugly. I saw you perching on the clock and muffling it with your wings, to keep it from striking loudly. Otherwise the mice would have been swept away. I heard what you shouted at Mouse King! Why didn't you help Nutcracker, why didn't you help me, you ugly Godfather Drosselmeier? Isn't it all your fault that I have to lie in bed, sick and injured?"

The mother, quite terrified, asked: "What's wrong with you, dear Marie?"

But Drosselmeier was making very bizarre faces and he spoke in a snarling and monotonous voice:

"Pendulum, had to hum, didn't wish to fit, clocks, clocks, clock pendulum, had to hum, softly hum, bells boom, bells blast, limp and lame and honk and hunk, doll girl, don't worry, scurry, ring the bell, bell is rung, bell is sung, to drive away Mouse King today, now the owl comes flying fast, pack and pick and pick and pack, chimes are jingly, clocks, hum, hum, pendulums have to hum, pick wouldn't stick, hum and hum and purr and purr!" Marie gaped at Godfather Drosselmeier because he looked very different and far uglier than usual, and because he kept swinging his right arm as if he were a marionette. She would have been truly horrified at the godfather if the mother hadn't been present, and if Fritz, having sneaked in, hadn't finally interrupted the godfather by laughing very loud.

"Oh, my, Godfather Drosselmeier! You're much too funny again today! You're gesticulating like my jumping jack, whom I tossed behind the stove long ago!"

The mother remained very earnest and she said: "Dear Herr Godfather, this is quite a strange joke. What are you aiming at?"

"Heavens!" retorted Drosselmeier, laughing. "Have you forgotten my charming clockmaker ditty? I always sing it for patients like Marie."

Now he settled at her bedside, saying:

"Just don't be angry that I didn't hack out all of Mouse King's fourteen eyes for you, but I couldn't have managed. Instead, I'll do something delightful for you."

Drosselmeier reached into his pocket and what he now softly, softly produced was: Nutcracker. The godfather had skillfully and solidly reinserted Nutcracker's lost teeth and straightened out his jaw.

Marie was utterly overjoyed, and Mother said, smiling:

"Now do you see that Godfather Drosselmeier means you no harm with your Nutcracker?"

"But Marie," the godfather broke in, "you must admit that Nutcracker doesn't actually have a great physique and that his face cannot exactly be called handsome. If you like, I can tell you how such ugliness came into his family and was handed down. Or do you happen to know the story of Princess Pirlipat, Mouserink's witch, and the artistic clockmaker?"

"Now listen," Fritz unexpectedly interrupted. "Listen, Godfather Drosselmeier. You inserted the teeth correctly in Nutcracker's mouth, and his jaw is no longer so wobbly. But why is he lacking a sword? Why didn't you give him a sword?"

"Oh, my," Drosselmeier retorted quite indignantly. "Why must you be grumpy and grouchy about everything, boy? What do I care about Nutcracker's sword? I healed his body—let him obtain a sword as he likes."

"You're right," cried Fritz. "He's a capable guy. He'll know where to find weapons!"

"Well, Marie," the godfather went on. "Do you know the tale of Princess Pirlipat?"

"No, I don't," Marie replied. "Tell us, dear Godfather, tell us!"

"I hope," said the mother, "I hope, dear Godfather, that your story won't be as gruesome as the stories you normally tell."

"By no means," answered Drosselmeier. "Quite the contrary! What I have the honor of reciting is quite humorous."

"Tell us, oh, tell us, Godfather!" cried the children, and Drosselmeier began.

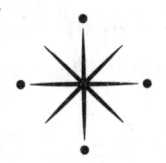

THE TALE OF THE HARD NUT

Pirlipat's mother was a king's wife, hence a queen, and in the moment of her birth, Pirlipat herself was a born princess. The king was beside himself for joy over his beautiful little daughter lying in the cradle. He exulted loudly, he danced and pranced on one leg, and he kept hollering, "Hurray! Has anybody ever seen anybody more beautiful?"

All the ministers, generals, presidents, magistrates, and staff officers hopped on one leg just like the sovereign and shouted: "No! Never!"

Indeed, there was no denying that no more beautiful child than Princess Pirlipat had been born since the dawn of time. Her little face was virtually woven out of lily-white and rosy red silk flakes, her little eyes were a vivid, sparkling azure, and her curls twisted in a full head of shiny gold threads. In addition, Pirlipat brought two rows of small pearly teeth into the world, and two hours later, when the grand chancellor tried to examine her facial lineaments more closely, she bit his finger so hard that he shrieked: "Oh, Jiminy!" Then again, others claim that he yelled, "Owww!" Opinions are sharply divided even today.

In any case, she really did bite the chancellor's finger, and now the delighted populace knew that intellect and intelligence dwelt inside Pirlipat's little body, which was as beautiful as that of an angel.

Everybody was delighted. Only the queen was very anxious and nervous

—no one knew why. What especially struck people was that she had the cradle guarded very carefully. Aside from the trabants who occupied every threshold, and aside from the pairs of ladies-in-waiting, who had to sit close to the cradle, six other ladies were scattered around the room, night by night.

However, what seemed quite foolish and unfathomable was that each of these six ladies-in-waiting had to take a tomcat in her lap and stroke him all night long, compelling him to ruminate constantly.

The Tale of the Hard Nut

It would be impossible, dear children, for you to guess why Pirlipat's mother made all these arrangements. But I know why and I will tell you now.

It happened that many very enchanting princes and marvelous kings had once gathered at the court of Pirlipat's father, which is why the entire court shone gleefully, and why countless plays, balls, and tournaments were put on. To show he didn't lack for gold and silver, the king wanted to thrust his hand properly into the royal treasury and lavish a decent amount. Having been secretly informed by the supreme royal kitchen master that the court astronomer had scheduled the slaughter of pigs, the king ordered a huge sausage feast. Then he jumped into the carriage and personally invited all the kings and princes himself—purely for a spoonful of soup, to enjoy the surprise of the magnificent delight.

Now the king spoke very amiably to the queen: "You know, my darling, how much I love sausages!"

The queen knew what the king was driving at. He meant simply that she ought to submit to the very useful business of making sausages, as she herself had done in the past.

The supreme treasurer had to promptly deliver the huge golden sausage cauldron and the silver casseroles to the kitchen. They lit a big sandalwood fire, the queen tied on her damask kitchen apron, and soon the sweet fragrances of the sausage soup were steaming out of the cauldron. The pungent aroma wafted all the way to the Privy Council.

The king, imbued with pleasure, couldn't help himself: "With your permission, gentlemen!" he shouted. He then flew into the kitchen, embraced the queen, stirred the soup with his gold scepter, and, calming down, he returned to the Privy Council.

They had reached the important point when the bacon was to be sliced into cubes and roasted on silver grills. The ladies-in-waiting left the kitchen because the queen wished to perform this action herself out of loyalty, fidelity, and devotion to the royal consort. However, when the bacon started to roast, they heard a very fine whispering: "Give me a little roast bacon, too, sister! I want to feast, too—after all, I'm a queen, too. Give me a bit of the roast bacon!"

The queen knew that Frau Mouserink was speaking. For many years now, she had been living in the royal palace. She claimed that she was related to the royal family, and that she herself was a queen in the land of Mousolia. And that was why she presided over a large court under the hearth. The queen was a good, charitable woman. If she didn't wish to recognize Frau Mouserink as queen and as her sister, then she could at least grant her, from the bottom of her heart, the banqueting on festive days. The queen exclaimed: "Come right out, Frau Mouserink. You can enjoy my bacon in any event!"

Frau Mouserink scurried over, hopping merrily. She leaped up to the hearth, and her delicate little paws took hold of each bit of bacon offered her by the queen.

But now all of Frau Mouserink's male and female relatives came springing up, as did her seven sons. These sons were ill-bred boors. They overwhelmed the bacon, and the terrified queen couldn't fend them off.

Luckily the royal controller's wife came running up. She drove away the intrusive guests, managing to leave some bacon, which, following the assessment of the royal mathematician, was distributed very skillfully among all the sausages.

With drums beating and trumpets blasting, all the visiting princes and potentates, clad in splendid holiday garb, drew past, heading toward the sausage feast, whereby some of the guests were mounted on white amblers, and some rode in crystal coaches. The king welcomed them with hearty friendship and benevolence; then, as sovereign, with his crown and his scepter, he sat down at the head of the table.

In the liverwurst station, people could see that the king was turning paler and paler, gazing at the heavens. Gentle moans fled his breast, a tremendous pain seemed to be burrowing through his insides! Then, in the blood sausage station, loudly groaning and groaning, weeping and wailing, he sank back in his armchair, with both hands over his face.

All the diners sprang up from the table, and the royal physician tried in vain to check the royal pulse—the king seemed to be ripped apart by a profound and nameless yowling. Finally, finally, after much coaxing, after the application of strong medicines, more than there were scorched quills, and so forth, the king seemed to have recovered somewhat. He barely stammered the words: "Too little bacon."

The queen now pathetically threw herself at his feet and cried out: "Oh, my poor, miserable royal consort! Oh, what pains you have suffered. But now you see the culprit at your feet! Punish, punish her hard! Ah, Frau Mouserink, with her seven sons and with all her male and female relatives, has gobbled up the bacon and—" But now the queen fell back in a dead faint.

The king furiously leaped up and yelled: "Royal controller's wife! How did it happen?"

The controller's wife reported whatever she knew, and the king resolved to get even with Frau Mouserink and her family for gobbling away the bacon from the sausages. The Privy Council assembled, and it decided to put Frau Mouserink on trial and to confiscate all her goods. However, the king pointed out that she could, after all, still gobble up the bacon during the procedure. So the entire matter was handed over to the royal clockmaker and the royal adept.

This man, who had the same name as I—namely, Christian Elias Drosselmeier—promised, through a very special, politically shrewd operation, to drive Frau Mouserink and her family out of the palace forever and ever. Drosselmeier actually invented very tiny, very skillful devices, in which roast bacon was applied to minuscule

The Tale of the Hard Nut

threads that Drosselmeier set up around the home of Frau Bacongobbler.

Frau Mouserink was far too wise not to catch Drosselmeier's cunning.

But none of her warnings, none of her notions could help. Lured by the sweet fragrance of the roast bacon, all of Frau Mouserink's seven sons and many, many male and female relatives stepped into Drosselmeier's devices; and just as they were about to nibble away the bacon, they were trapped by a suddenly dropping gate and then shamefully executed right in the kitchen.

With her tiny squad, Frau Mouserink abandoned the site of terror. Grief, despair, and revenge imbued her breast. The court rejoiced heartily, but the queen was worried, for she was well acquainted with Frau Mouserink's mentality and she knew that Frau Mouserink would not leave the deaths of her sons and relatives unavenged. And indeed, Frau Mouserink did appear just as the queen was preparing a lung puree for the royal consort—a treat he especially liked. And Frau Mouserink said:

"My sons, my relatives have been killed. Be careful, Your Royal Highness, make sure that Mouse Queen doesn't chew the little princess in half—make sure."

Thereupon she vanished again and was seen no more. But the queen was so terrified that she dropped the lung puree into the fire; and so Frau Mouserink spoiled a second royal treat, which infuriated the king.

****

"But that's enough for Fritz and Marie tonight. The rest will be taken care of tomorrow."

Marie had her own thoughts in regard to the story, and much as she asked Godfather Drosselmeier to keep going, she didn't wait to be persuaded.

Instead, she jumped up: "Too much of a good thing is unhealthy—we'll hear the final part of the story tomorrow."

Just as the counselor was about to step out the front door, Fritz asked: "Do tell me, Godfather Drosselmeier, is it really true that you invented the mousetrap?"

"How can you ask such a silly question?" the mother cried. But the godfather smiled inscrutably and he murmured: "Am I not enough of a skillful clockmaker and not even enough to invent mousetraps?"

CONTINUATION
OF THE TALE OF THE HARD NUT

Now you know very well, children (Drosselmeier continued the next evening), you know very well why the queen had the gorgeous Princess Pirlipat guarded so carefully. Shouldn't the queen fear that Frau Mouserink might carry out her threats, come back, and chew the little princess to death? Drosselmeier's devices were useless against Frau Mouserink's wisdom and insight; and only the royal astronomer, who also doubled as the king's secret diviner and stargazer, appeared to know that only the family of Tomcat Purr would be able to keep Frau Mouserink away from the cradle of the princess. Hence it happened that each lady-in-waiting held one of the sons of that family in her lap, deftly stroking him, trying to sweeten his vast political service. Incidentally, the sons were employed at court as secret legation counsels.

One midnight, one of the two ladies sitting close to the cradle awoke out of deep sleep. Everybody around them lay there, trapped by slumber—no purring, a deep and deathly hush, in which the picking of the woodworm could be heard! But how did the secret supreme lady-in-waiting feel when she spotted a huge, hideous mouse, which stood up on its hind legs, pressing its wretched face against the head of the princess?

With a shriek of dismay, the lady jumped up. Everybody awoke. That same moment, Frau Mouserink (nobody else was the big mouse on Pirlipat's cradle) scurried into a corner of the room. The legation counsels dashed after her. But too late. Frau Mouserink vanished through a crack in the floor. Pirlipat was awakened by the uproar and she wept very lamentably.

"Thank goodness!" the ladies exclaimed. "She's alive!"

But how great was their horror when they looked for Pirlipat and saw what had become of the lovely, delicate child. Instead of her golden locks with a red and white face and an angelic head, a thick, deformed head now perched on a twisted, teensy-weensy body. The small azure eyes had turned into green, gaping, gawking eyes, and the little lips had pulled from one ear to the other.

The queen dissolved in weeping and wailing, and the royal study had to be thoroughly padded because time after time the king would run with his head against the wall, shouting lamentably: "Oh, what a miserable monarch I am!"

The king realized perfectly well that it would have been better to eat the sausages without bacon and leave Frau Mouserink and her clan in peace behind the hearth. But Pirlipat's royal father wouldn't hear of it. Instead, he placed all the blame on the royal clockmaker and adept, Christian Elias Drosselmeier from Nuremberg. That was why the king issued a wise order: Drosselmeier had four weeks to restore Princess Pirlipat to her former condition or at least indicate a specific, unerring measure for doing so.

Otherwise, the royal clockmaker would be doomed to a shameful death under the headsman's ax.

Drosselmeier was not without fear, but he relied on his skill and his luck, and he promptly tackled the first operation that struck him as useful. He took Princess Pirlipat apart very adroitly, unscrewed her little hands and feet, and viewed her inner structure. But, alas, he found that the bigger the princess grew, the more shapeless she became, and he was at a loss—at his wit's end. He very carefully put her together again and sank into a melancholy at her cradle, which he was not allowed to leave.

The fourth week had already begun. It was Wednesday when the king peered into the cradle, his eyes sparkling furiously. Brandishing his scepter, the king exclaimed: "Christian Elias Drosselmeier, cure the princess, or you must die!" Drosselmeier started weeping bitterly, but the princess delightfully cracked nuts.

For the first time, Drosselmeier noticed that Pirlipat had been born with teeth and that she had an unusual appetite for nuts. Indeed, she had hollered so long after her transformation, until a nut happened to come her way. She promptly cracked it open, ate the kernel, and then calmed down. Since then, the ladies couldn't bring her enough nuts.

"Oh, holy instinct of nature, eternally inscrutable sympathy of all beings," cried Christian Elias Drosselmeier, "you show me the gates to the mystery. I wish to knock, and the gates will open." Drosselmeier then asked for permission to speak to the court astronomer, and he was taken to him under heavy guard. These two gentlemen embraced tearfully because they were close friends. Next they withdrew into a secret study, where they perused many books dealing with instincts, sympathies, antipathies, and other mysterious things.

Night broke in. The court astronomer gazed at the stars and, with the help of the very dexterous Drosselmeier, he cast the princess's horoscope. This demanded great effort, for the lines got more and more entangled. But finally—what joy. Finally it lay clearly before them that the princess, in order to undo the hideous spell and restore her beauty, had nothing to do but enjoy the sweet Krakatuk Nut.

The shell of the Krakatuk Nut was so hard that a forty-eight-pound cannon could have charged across it without breaking it. But this hard nut had to be chewed up in front of the princess by a man who had never shaved and who had never worn boots. And with closed eyes, he handed the princess the kernel. The young man could reopen his eyes only after taking seven steps backward without stumbling.

Drosselmeier and the astronomer labored uninterruptedly for three days and three nights. Now the king was having his Saturday dinner. All at once, Drosselmeier, who was to be decapitated on Sunday, at the crack of dawn, burst in joyfully and ecstatically and he announced the measure for restoring the princess's lost beauty. The king hugged Drosselmeier with intense benevolence and promised him a diamond sword, four medals, and two new Sunday coats.

"After we finish our meal," the king added amiably, "we can get to work right away. Make sure, dear adept, that the young unshaven and nonbooted man with the Krakatuk Nut is properly at hand. He should drink no wine earlier; otherwise he'll stumble when he tries taking seven steps backward like a crab. Afterward he can liquor up for all he's worth!"

Drosselmeier was stunned by the king's words, and it was not without shaking and shuddering that he managed to squeeze out a response: he had discovered the measure. Now both the Krakatuk Nut and the young man had to be sought. But it remained doubtful whether Nut and Nutcracker could ever be found.

The fuming sovereign swung his scepter over his crowned head and he roared in a lion's voice: "Then we'll make do with your heads!"

Luckily for Drosselmeier, who was filled with terror and misery, the king had found his meal to be delicious that very day. So he was in the right mood to listen to reasonable ideas, of which the magnanimous queen had no lack.

Indeed, she was deeply touched by Drosselmeier's fate. Drosselmeier pulled himself together and finally pointed out that he had gained his life by actually carrying out the king's orders. He had been told to find the means of curing the princess and he had done so.

The king called these lame excuses and silly twaddle. But eventually, after drinking a glass of digestive, he decided that both the clockmaker and the astronomer should get going and should not return without a Krakatuk Nut in their pocket. The man who bit them open should, as the queen informed them, insert multiple public notices and various advertisements in domestic and foreign gazettes.

***

Drosselmeier broke off here and he promised to finish the story tomorrow evening.

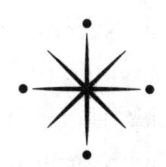

CONCLUSION OF THE TALE
OF THE HARD NUT

No sooner were the lights lit on the following evening than Godfather Drosselmeier actually showed up and continued the story.

Drosselmeier and the court astronomer had been roaming for fifteen years already without catching even a hint of the Krakatuk Nut. Now I could spend four whole weeks telling you, dear children, where they had been and what strange things they had encountered. But I won't report on those matters. I'll merely say that in his deep sorrow, Drosselmeier eventually felt deeply homesick for his dear hometown of Nuremberg. This yearning swept over him especially one day when he and his friend happened to be in a vast, Asian forest, smoking pipes filled with cheap tobacco.

"Oh, beautiful, beautiful hometown of Nuremberg—beautiful town. If a person hasn't seen you, even though he may have traveled a lot, to London, Paris, Petrovaradin, then his heart cannot have surged. He must long for you always, long for you, oh, Nuremberg, beautiful town with its beautiful houses and windows."

When Drosselmeier lamented so dolefully, the astronomer was filled with profound commiseration, and he started to bawl so deplorably that his weeping and wailing could be heard all over Asia. But then he pulled himself together, wiped the tears from his eyes, and asked:

"Worthy colleague, why do we sit here and blubber? Why don't we go to Nuremberg? Does it really matter where and how we seek the wretched Krakatuk Nut?"

"That's true," Drosselmeier replied in comfort.

The two men stood up, knocked the tobacco from their pipes, and headed straight out of the Asian forest toward Nuremberg. No sooner had they arrived, than Drosselmeier hurried over to visit his cousin, the doll maker, lacquerer, and gilder Christoph Zacharias Drosselmeier, whom he hadn't seen for many, many years.

The clockmaker told his cousin the entire story about Princess Pirlipat, Frau Mouserink, and the Krakatuk Nut.

Conclusion of the Tale of the Hard Nut

Time and again, the cousin threw his hands together and cried out in amazement: "Oh, cousin, cousin, what wondrous things these are!"

Drosselmeier kept talking about his adventures on his vast travels. He had spent two years with the date king, had been disdainfully rejected by the almond prince, and had inquired in vain at the Nature Society in Eichhornshausen. In short, the clockmaker had failed everywhere to find even a trace of the Krakatuk Nut.

During this account, Christoph Zacharias had often snapped his fingers, whirled around on one foot, clicked his tongue, and cried out: "Hm, hm, I, Ei, O—the devil take it!" Finally, he threw his cap and his wig into the air, and hugged and squeezed the cousin. "Cousin, cousin! You are safe and you are sound, I tell you, for everything and everyone must be deceiving me if I don't own the Krakatuk Nut myself!"

He then produced a box, from which he drew a gilt nut of medium size. "Look," he said, showing the nut to his cousin. "Look! Let me tell you about this nut."

***

Many Christmases ago, a stranger came here, peddling a sack of nuts. Unfortunately, he got into a fight with the local nut dealer right outside my doll's cottage; so he put down his sack in order to defend himself more easily. The resident attacked the stranger because he couldn't stand having the outsider hawk nuts. At that moment, a heavily loaded truck rolled over the sack, crushing all the nuts but one, which the stranger, with a bizarre smile, offered me for a shiny twenty-penny piece from the year 1720. This struck me as wonderful. Now I happened to have such a coin in my pocket. I bought the nut and gilded it, not quite knowing why I had paid so much and why I now held the nut in such high esteem.

This was definitely the Krakatuk Nut that they had been hunting; any doubts were dispelled when they summoned the astronomer, and he scraped the gilt cleanly off with the coin. Under the gilt, they found the word "Krakatuk" engraved in Chinese characters.

The travelers were ecstatic, and the cousin was the happiest man under the sun when Drosselmeier assured him that his fortune was made. Aside from a considerable pension, he would receive for free all gold for gilding. Both the adept and the astronomer had already put on their nightcaps and were about to hop into bed when the astronomer began: "My dear colleague, all good things come in pairs. We have found not only the Krakatuk Nut, but also the young man who bites her open and hands the beauty of the kernel to the princess. I mean nobody other than your own cousin's son. No! I don't want to sleep, I want to cast the boy's horoscope tonight!" Next the astronomer tore the nightcap off the boy's head and he began to observe the stars.

The boy was actually nice and well built, and he had never shaved and he had never worn boots. Granted, in

Conclusion of the Tale of the Hard Nut

his early youth, he had been a jumping jack for about two weeks; but now there wasn't even the slightest inkling of that time, for he had been educated through his father's efforts. During the Yule season, he wore a lovely, gold-trimmed red coat and a sword. He kept his hat under his arm and he sported an excellent hairstyle and a bagwig. Now he stood, glowing, in his father's chamber, and, out of native gallantry, he cracked the nuts for the young girls, which is why they had nicknamed him Dear Little Nutcracker.

The next morning, the ecstatic astronomer threw his arms around the adept and shouted: "He's the one! We've got him, we've found him! But there are two things, dearest colleague, that we mustn't ignore. First of all, you have to braid your wonderful nephew a robust, wooden queue, which is linked so closely to the lower jaw that the latter can be strongly pulled. Now when we arrive at the residence, we must cautiously hide the fact that we have brought along the young man who bites open the Krakatuk Nut. Quite the contrary! He has to turn up a great deal later than we.

"According to the horoscope, several men have gnashed up a few teeth unsuccessfully, and so the king has promised that the suitor who chews up the nut and restores Pirlipat's beauty will be rewarded with the hand of the princess and with the right of succession to the throne."

The doll maker cousin was quite satisfied that his boy should marry Princess Pirlipat and become prince and king, so he left him fully to the envoy. The queue that Drosselmeier braided for his young, hopeful nephew was so admirable that he put on the most brilliant experiments by chewing up the hardest peach pits.

Drosselmeier and the astronomer promptly informed the authorities of their discovery of the Krakatuk Nut, whereby the necessary arrangements were made on the spot. And when the travelers arrived with the cosmetic preparation, many attractive people, including even a few princes, had already appeared. Relying on their healthy teeth, they wanted to break the spell cast on the princess.

The envoys were horrified when they saw the princess. The tiny body with its teensy hands and feet could barely carry the shapeless head. The ugliness of the face was increased by a white cotton beard around the mouth and the chin.

Now everything occurred just as the court astronomer had read in the horoscope. Clad in shoes, one young shaver after another bit himself sore on the Krakatuk's teeth and jowls without helping the princess in the least. Dentists had been summoned, and when an unfortunate suitor was being carried away half unconscious, he would sigh: "That was a hard nut to crack!"

Now when the king, in the terror of his heart, promised his daughter and his kingdom to the suitor who would cast off the magic spell, the gentle cousin stepped forward and asked permission to start the process. Nobody but the young Drosselmeier appealed

Conclusion of the Tale of the Hard Nut

so intently to Princess Pirlipat. She placed her tiny hands on her heart and sighed quite tenderly: "Ah! If only he'll be the one who bites open the Krakatuk Nut and becomes my husband!"

After young Drosselmeier very politely bowed to the king and the queen and also Princess Pirlipat, he received the Krakatuk Nut from the hands of the supreme master of ceremonies. Taking the nut between his teeth, the boy tugged at his queue and—crack, crack, crack—the shell crumbled into many bits and pieces. Adroitly the boy cleaned the threads still dangling from the kernel and handed it over to the princess, while bowing and scraping, whereupon he closed his eyes and began stepping backward. The princess then swallowed the kernel and—oh wonder!—the freak vanished and instead there stood a woman of angelic beauty. Her face was virtually woven out of silk flakes that were lily-white and rosy red. Her eyes were like glowing azure, her full locks curling as if twisting like golden threads. Drums and trumpets joined the loud jubilation of the people. The king with his entire court danced on one leg as they had done at Pirlipat's birth; and the queen had to be revived with eau de cologne because she had fainted in bliss and pleasure.

Young Drosselmeier hadn't even completed his seven steps when the tumult disrupted his self-composure; but he held out for self-control. He was just sticking out his right foot for his seventh pace, when Frau Mouserink, hideously squeaking and squealing, rose out of the floor.

As a result, Drosselmeier, about to set down his own foot, stepped so hard on Frau Mouserink's foot that he stumbled and almost lurched over.

"Oh, misfortune!"

In the blink of an eye, the boy became as misshapen as the princess had been. His body was shrunken, and it could barely carry the thick, malformed head with its huge, bulging eyes and its broad, dreadfully yawning maw.

Instead of the queue, a narrow, wooden cape hung down his back, thereby controlling the lower jaw.

The clockmaker and the astronomer were beside themselves with dismay and horror. But then they saw Frau Mouserink bleeding and rolling on the floor. Her evil did not go unavenged, for young Drosselmeier had struck her throat so roughly with the sharp heel of his shoe that she was doomed to expire, and in peril of death, she squeaked and squealed lamentably:

"Oh, Krakatuk, hard nut, see, the death of me. Hee hee, pee pee! Fine little Nutcracker, soon you too will be dead for all to see. Seven crowns for seven heads, Mother will pronounce you dead, Nutcracker fine will be all mine. Oh, life so fresh and red, I leave you dead! Squeal!" With that shriek, Frau Mouserink gave up the ghost, and her corpse was carried off by the royal oven heater.

Nobody had paid any heed to young Drosselmeier, but now the princess reminded the king of his promise. And so he immediately sent for the young hero. But when the unhappy boy stepped forward in his deformity,

Conclusion of the Tale of the Hard Nut

the princess held both hands over her face and yelled, "Away, away with the wretched Nutcracker!" The Lord Chamberlain grabbed the boy's little shoulders and threw him out the door.

The king was furious that they had tried to force a Nutcracker on him as his son-in-law. He blamed everything on the misfortune of the clockmaker and the astronomer and he barred them from ever stepping foot inside the residence again.

None of this was mentioned in the horoscope that the astronomer had cast in Nuremberg. But it didn't prevent him from observing the heavens once more. And indeed he read a number of things in the stars. He found that young Drosselmeier would do so well in his new position that he would become prince and king despite his malformation. However, his deformity would vanish only when Frau Mouserink's son—whom she had borne after the deaths of her seven sons with seven heads—had become Mouse King. That son would have to be felled by his own hand, and a lady would have to fall in love with him despite his defects. Indeed, around Christmas, young Drosselmeier had supposedly been spotted in his father's chamber in Nuremberg—granted, as Nutcracker, yet definitely as prince!

***

"That, children, is the tale of the hard nut. And now you know why people are apt to say: 'That was a hard nut to crack.' And now you know why Nutcrackers are so hideous." And that was how Drosselmeier concluded his story.

Marie felt that Princess Pirlipat was really a loathsome and ungrateful thing.

Fritz, on the contrary, assured her that if Nutcracker was otherwise a decent sort, he wouldn't beat around the bush with Mouse King, and he would soon regain his earlier good looks.

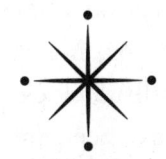

UNCLE AND NEPHEW

If any one of my highly esteemed readers or listeners has ever accidentally cut himself on broken glass, he will personally know how painful it is, and how awful it is altogether since it heals so slowly. Marie had to spend nearly a whole week in bed because she felt so dizzy whenever she stood up. But finally she was hale and hearty again, as ever, springing all about the room. The inside of the glass cabinet looked very appealing since trees and blossoms and houses and lovely, glowing dolls stood there, new and shiny.

Above all, Marie found her dear Nutcracker, who, erect on the second shelf, smiled at her with sound little teeth. When she gazed at her favorite to her heart's content, she suddenly felt very agitated. She saw everything Godfather Drosselmeier had told them—especially the story of Nutcracker and his quarrel with Frau Mouserink and her son.

Now Marie realized that her Nutcracker could be none other than young Drosselmeier from Nuremberg—the likable nephew, who, alas, was hexed by Frau Mouserink. As the tale was being told, Marie didn't doubt for even an instant that the skillful clockmaker at the court of Pirlipat's father could have been anyone else but Godfather Drosselmeier himself. "But why didn't Uncle help you? Why didn't he help you?"

That was Marie's lament, and it raged livelier and livelier inside her, while the battle she was watching focused on Nutcracker's crown and kingdom. Weren't then all the other dolls his subjects, and wasn't it then certain that the astronomer's prophecy had come true, and that young Drosselmeier had become king of the kingdom of dolls? In properly weighing all these matters, wise Marie also believed that Nutcracker and his vassals had actually started living the moment she entrusted them with life and motion.

But that wasn't the case. The figures in the cabinet remained stationary and motionless. And Marie, far from giving up her inner conviction, put the blame on the still effective spell cast by Frau Mouserink and her seven-headed son.

"Well, dear Herr Drosselmeier," Marie spoke aloud to Nutcracker. "You may not be able to move or to speak. But I'm well aware that you understand me and that you fully know my good intentions with you. Count on my aid if you need it. At least, I want to ask my uncle to lend a helping hand when his skill calls for it."

Nutcracker remained still and quiet. But Marie felt as if a gentle sigh were breathing through the glass cabinet, whereby the panes resounded—barely audible, but wondrously charming—and a faint chimelike voice appeared to be singing: "Little Marie, my guardian angel be! Yours I will be, my Marie!" The girl felt a strange comfort in the icy shudders that flashed through her body. Twilight had arrived. The medical officer and Godfather Drosselmeier came into the room, and it wasn't long before Luise had set the tea table, and the family sat around, talking about all kinds of cheerful things. Marie had very quietly brought in her little armchair and settled at Drosselmeier's feet. Now when everybody held their tongue, Marie peered into Drosselmeier's face with her big, blue eyes, and she said:

"I now know, dear Godfather, that my Nutcracker is really your nephew, young Drosselmeier from Nuremberg. He has become prince or rather king—all this has come true as was predicted by his companion, the astronomer. But you also know that he is on a war footing with the ugly Mouse King, the son of Frau Mouserink. Why don't you help him?"

Marie then retold the entire account of the battle as she had witnessed it. She was often interrupted by the noisy laughter of Luise and the mother. Only Fritz and Drosselmeier remained earnest.

"Just where does the girl get all her nonsense from?" said the medical officer.

"Goodness," the mother replied. "Why, she's got a lively imagination.

These are just dreams created by her ardent fever."

"None of this is true," said Fritz. "My red Hussars aren't such cowards!

Goodness, gracious me! Darn it all! How else would I come down?"

With a bizarre smile, Godfather Drosselmeier took Marie on his lap and spoke more gently than ever:

"Why, dear Marie, you've been given more than I, than any of us. Like Pirlipat, you are a native-born princess, for you rule a bright and lovely kingdom. But you'll have to suffer a lot if you want to take charge of poor, deformed Nutcracker, since Mouse King persecutes him anywhere and everywhere. However, I'm not the one who can save him! Only you can rescue him. Be strong and loyal."

Neither Marie nor anybody else knew what Drosselmeier meant. Instead, the medical officer found those words so strange that he checked Drosselmeier's pulse: "Most worthy friend, you have a serious case of cerebral congestion. Let me write you a prescription."

But the mother thoughtfully shook her head and murmured: "I can catch Godfather Drosselmeier's drift, but I can't articulate it clearly."

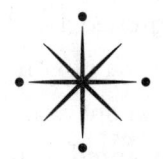

VICTORY

It wasn't long before Marie was awakened by a tapping in the moonlit night—a strange knocking that seemed to originate in a corner of the room. It sounded like small stones being hurled and rolled to and fro, with a quite repulsive squeaking and squealing in between.

"Ah! The mice, the mice are returning!" Marie shouted in horror, and she tried to wake up her mother. But every sound stuck in her throat. Indeed, she couldn't stir at all when she saw Mouse King burrowing his way through a hole in the wall. With sparkling eyes and crowns, he then scurried about the room. Finally, with a tremendous jump, he landed on the nightstand right at Marie's bedside: "Hee, hee, hee, you must give me your sugar peas, your marzipan—see! Otherwise I'll chew up your Nutcracker, hee—your Nutcracker, see!" That was Mouse King, hideously munching and crunching with his teeth; and then he swiftly jumped back through the hole.

Marie was so frightened by the gruesome spectacle that when she woke up the next morning, she was utterly pale, and so agitated that she was unable to utter a word. A hundred times, she wanted to tell her mother or Luise or at least Fritz what had happened to her. But then she thought: "Will anyone believe me, and won't they laugh their heads off in the bargain?" But one thing was clear. In order to save Nutcracker, she would have to hand over her sugar peas and her marzipan.

That evening, she took as many of those supplies as she had, and she placed them on the ledge of the cabinet. The next morning her mother said: "I just don't know where the mice are coming from in our living room. Look at poor Marie! They've gobbled up all your sweets!"

And it was true. The greedy Mouse King didn't much care for filled marzipan, but he had gnawed on it with his sharp teeth, so that it had to be thrown away. Marie shrugged off the loss of the sweets; she was so delighted that, as she believed, her Nutcracker was saved.

Still, how did she feel the following night when the squeaking and squealing were right on her ears? Ah, Mouse King was back. His eyes sparkled more dreadfully than on the previous night, and the whistling between his teeth was even more repulsive.

"You have to give me your sugar dolls and your tragacanth dolls, you little thing. Otherwise, you little thing, I'll chew up your Nutcracker, your Nutcracker!" And the gruesome Mouse King sped away!

The next morning, Marie was very sad as she went over to the cabinet and most dolefully gazed at her sugar and tragacanth dolls. But her pain was valid. For, my attentive listener, Marie, you may not believe what loving figures shaped out of sugar and tragacanth belonged to little Marie Stahlbaum.

Next to her, a very handsome shepherd with a shepherdess was grazing an entire herd of milk white lambs, accompanied by his bold little dog. There were also two postmen carrying mail, and four very attractive couples—cleanly dressed youths with wonderfully clad girls swinging in Russian swings. Behind several dancers stood the Maid of Orleans, by whom Marie didn't set much store. But deep in the corner there stood a red-cheeked boy, Marie's favorite, and the tears poured out of her eyes.

"Ah," she cried, turning to Nutcracker. "Dear Drosselmeier, what wouldn't I do to save you? But it's so very difficult!"

Meanwhile, Nutcracker looked so tearful that—as if seeing Mouse King's seven jaws wide open and aiming at devouring the miserable youth—Marie decided to sacrifice everything. Hence, that evening, she placed all the sweet dolls, just as she had placed the sweets, on the ridge of the glass cabinet. She kissed the shepherd, the shepherdess, and the lambs. Then she finally brought her favorite, the little red-cheeked child of the tragacanth, from the corner, and she slipped him all the way back. The Maid of Orleans had to be moved to the first row.

"No! This is too awful!" the mother exclaimed the next morning. "Some huge, nasty mouse must be wreaking havoc in the glass cabinet, for all of Marie's beautiful sugar dolls have been gnawed on and nibbled on." Marie couldn't help weeping, but she soon smiled again, for she thought to herself: "What does it matter? Nutcracker's been saved!"

In the evening, the mother told Drosselmeier about the mischief worked by a mouse in the children's cabinet. "It's appalling that we can't destroy the obnoxious mouse that's acting up in the glass cabinet, gobbling away poor Marie's sweets."

"Goodness," Fritz broke in cheerfully. "The baker downstairs has a fabulous gray cat. I'll bring him here. He'll soon put an end to the issue and bite off the mouse's head—whether it's Frau Mouserink herself or her son, Mouse King."

"And," the mother went on with a laugh, "the cat

will jump around on chairs and tables and throw down cups and glasses and commit a thousand other kinds of mayhem."

"Oh, not at all!" Fritz retorted. "The baker's cat is very deft. I wish I could climb up to the tip of the roof as delicately as that cat."

"Just no tomcat at night," said Luise, who couldn't stand cats.

"Actually," said the medical officer, "actually, Fritz is right. Meanwhile

we can set a trap! Don't we have one?"

"Godfather Drosselmeier can do the best job," said Fritz.

"After all, he invented the mousetrap!" Everyone laughed.

When the mother assured them that no trap was to be found in the house, Drosselmeier announced that he owned several. He went home and an hour later he returned with an excellent mousetrap. Now the godfather's tale of the hard nut grew lively, even apparent for Fritz and Marie. When the cook was roasting the bacon, Marie shivered and shuddered.

Fully imbued with the tale and its marvels, she said to well-known Dore: "Ah, my queen! Just watch out for Frau Mouserink and her family."

Fritz, however, had drawn his sword: "Yes! Just let them come! I'll teach them a thing or two." But everybody under and on the hearth remained calm.

Now when Drosselmeier tied the bacon to a fine thread and gently, gently placed the trap next to the glass cabinet, Fritz exclaimed: "Be careful, clockmaker, don't let Mouse King play any tricks on you!"

Oh, how miserable Marie was the following night! Her arm was ice-cold, she moved to and fro, her cheeks were raw and wretched, and the squealing and squeaking filled her ears. The repugnant Mouse King sat on her shoulder, and he driveled, bloodred, out of the seven gaping maws. And with munching and crunching teeth, he hissed into Marie's ear, hissed with terror and horror!

"Hiss out, hiss out, don't enter the house, don't join the feast—that went to the trap! Hiss out, hiss out, hand over, hand over, all your picture books, plus the dress, plus no rest! Just for you to know, poor Nutcracker will miss all night, he'll bite out of sight! Hee, hee, dee, dee, squeal, squeak!"

Marie was filled with sadness and sorrow. The next morning, she looked quite pale and bewildered when her mother said: "The wicked mouse still hasn't been caught!" Believing that Marie was mourning her sweets and was also scared of the mouse, the mother added: "But just keep calm, dear child, we'll soon drive away the nasty mouse. If the traps don't work, then Fritz will bring his gray cat."

No sooner was Marie alone in the living room than she went over to the glass cabinet and sobbed to Nutcracker: "Ah, my dear, good Herr Drosselmeier! What can I, a poor, unhappy girl, do for you? I can also give away all my picture books and even my lovely new dress that was given to me by Holy Christ. I can hand over that horrid Mouse King for him to chew me up. But no matter how much I give him, Mouse King will keep asking for more and more until I've got nothing left and he ultimately chews me up instead of you. Oh, I, poor child, just what should I do? Just what should I do?"

While grieving and bereaving, little Marie noticed that a large bloodstain was left over from that night, from Nutcracker. Ever since Marie learned that her Nutcracker was actually young Drosselmeier's nephew, she stopped carrying him on her arm, stopped hugging and kissing the boy. Indeed, she barely touched him because of a certain timidity.

But now, she removed him very cautiously from the shelf and she started rubbing away the bloodstain with her handkerchief. Suddenly, however, she felt that Nutcracker was growing warm in her hand and beginning to stir. She swiftly returned him to his shelf. Her lips shook to and fro and she arduously whispered to Nutcracker.

"Ah, most worthy Demoiselle Stahlbaum, excellent friend, how much I owe you. No, you won't sacrifice any picture book for me, any dress given you by Christ. Just get me a sword, a sword, and I'll take care of the rest. May he—" Here, Nutcracker lost his power of speech, and his eyes, inspired to express the inmost melancholy, became frozen and lifeless again. Marie experienced no horror.

Rather, she hopped for joy since she knew of a method for saving Nutcracker without further painful sacrifices. But where would they get a sword for the boy?

Marie decided to ask Fritz for advice. So in the evening, when their parents had gone out, the two children sat alone in the living room, by the glass cabinet. And here she told her brother everything that had happened to her with Nutcracker and with Mouse King, and why it was necessary to save Nutcracker. Fritz grew more pensive over nothing so much as—according to Marie's report— his Hussars had conducted themselves so poorly in the battle. He again asked very earnestly if that was true, and when Marie assured him that it was indeed true, Fritz hurried over to the glass cabinet. There he gave a grandiloquent speech. Then, to punish their selfishness and cowardice, he cut off the ensigns from their caps one by one. Furthermore, he forbade them from blaring the Hussar March for a whole year.

After pronouncing his sentence, Fritz turned back to Marie, saying: "As for a sword, I can help Nutcracker. Yesterday I pensioned off an old colonel of the Cuirassiers. He won't be needing his sharp and lovely saber any longer."

The colonel consumed the pension allotted to him by Fritz, who kept him in the back most corner of the third shelf in the cabinet. He was drawn up from there, the decorated silver sword taken off and hung around Nutcracker.

Victory

The following night, Marie was still so horrified that she couldn't fall asleep. Around midnight, it sounded as if a bizarre racket, a roaring and jangling came from the living room. All at once, there was a squeal! "Mouse King! Mouse King!" cried Marie, and, horrified, she jumped out of bed.

Everyone remained still. But soon there was a soft, soft tapping on the door, and a very fine voice was heard:

"Most esteemed Demoiselle Stahlbaum! You don't have to worry about opening up—I've got good, cheerful news!" Marie recognized the voice of young Drosselmeier. She tossed her little coat on and flung open the door. Little Nutcracker was standing outside, with his bloody sword in his right hand and a wax candle in his left hand. Upon spotting Marie, he knelt down on one knee and said:

"You, oh lady, you alone have steeled me with chivalrous courage and have strengthened my arm in order to fight the boisterous man who has dared to scorn you. The treacherous Mouse King has been defeated and he is now rolling in his own blood! Oh, lady! Do not refuse to accept the signs of victory from the hand of your knight, who is devoted to you even unto death." With these words, little Nutcracker very skillfully tripped off the seven golden crowns of Mouse King, which he had slipped over his left arm. He handed the seven crowns to Marie, who joyfully received them.

Nutcracker stood up and continued speaking:

"Ah, my dearest Demoiselle Stahlbaum! Having overpowered my enemy, I ask you: What could I do to show you splendid things—if you felt enough affection for me to take just a few steps! Oh, do it, do it—my dearest demoiselle."

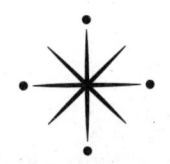

THE KINGDOM OF DOLLS

I believe that none of you children would have hesitated for even an instant to obey honest and kindhearted Nutcracker, who could never have had anything nasty in mind. As for Marie, she was all the more obedient since she knew how greatly she could rely on Nutcracker's gratitude. Indeed, she was convinced that he would keep his word and show her many splendid things.

She therefore said: "I'll go with you, Herr Drosselmeier. But it mustn't be far or last a long time. You see, I didn't get enough sleep last night."

"That," replied Nutcracker, "is why I'm taking the nearest path, although it's somewhat difficult."

He took the lead, followed by Marie, until he stopped by the huge, old wardrobe in the hallway. Marie was astonished to see that the doors of this closet, normally shut, were now wide open, so that she clearly made out her father's traveling fox fur, which hung in front. Nutcracker very deftly climbed up the ridges and adornments so that he could get hold of the enormous tassel, which, fastened by a thick cord, hung on the back of that fur. When Nutcracker pulled hard on the tassel, a very delicate cedar stairway quickly dropped through the fur sleeve.

"Please go up, dearest demoiselle," cried Nutcracker.

Marie did so, but scarcely had she gone up through the sleeve, scarcely had she peered out of the collar, than a blinding light shone toward her. All at once, she found herself on a marvelously fragrant meadow, from which millions of sparks arose like blinking gems.

"We're on the Rock Candy Meadow," said Nutcracker. "But soon we'll pass through that gate."

Now, looking up, Marie first noticed the lovely gate just a few steps forward on the meadow. The gate seemed to be made of white, brown, and raisin-colored sprinkled marble. But when Marie drew closer, she saw that the entire mass consisted of baked raisins and sugared almonds. That was why, as Nutcracker assured her, the gate they were passing through was called the Almond and Raisin Gate. Common folk very indecorously nicknamed it the Snack Gate.

In a gallery of this gateway, obviously made of barley sugar, six monkeys in red jerkins were playing the most beautiful Turkish military music. As a result, Marie scarcely noticed that she was progressing farther and farther on multicolored tiles, which, however, were nothing but nicely filled lozenges. Soon the travelers were surrounded by the sweetest perfumes, which poured out of a wondrous grove that opened on both sides. In the dark foliage, the interior glowed and gleamed so brightly that you could see gold and silver fruits hanging on gaudy branches. Stems and stalks had decorated themselves with ribbons and bouquets like merry marital couples and cheerful wedding guests. And when the orange scents billowed like zephyrs, then the twigs and leaves all hummed, and the tinsel flapped and fluttered so thoroughly that it all sounded like jubilant music, which had to accompany the sparkling lights, the hopping and dancing.

"Ah, how beautiful it all is!" cried Marie, blissful and enraptured.

"We're in Christmas Forest, my dear demoiselle," said Nutcracker. "Ah," Marie continued. "If only I could spend a little time here—oh, it's far too beautiful!"

Nutcracker clapped his little hands, and along came a few small shepherds and shepherdesses, hunters and huntswomen, who were so white and tender that you could have believed them to be pure sugar, that Marie had not yet noticed, even though they had been strolling in the woods. They brought over a favorite gold armchair, placed a white cushion of licorice upon it, and very courteously invited Marie to settle down. No sooner had she done so than shepherds and shepherdesses came and danced a very pretty ballet, whereby the hunters blew their instruments quite decently. But then they all vanished in the bushes.

"Forgive me," said Nutcracker, "forgive me, dearest Demoiselle Stahlbaum, for doing such a miserable dance. You see, the dancers all came from our marionette ballet, which is controlled by wires, and which can only do the same things over and over again. There are also good reasons why the hunters were so drowsy and feeble in their blowing. The sugar basket does hang at nose level on the Christmas tree, but it's still too high. Well, why don't we stroll a bit more?"

"Ah, everything was very lovely, and I really liked it!" said Marie, standing up and following Nutcracker. They walked along a murmuring, sweetly whispering brook, which seemed to be filling the forest with all of its marvelous scents.

"This is Orange Brook," said Nutcracker when asked. "It has a lovely fragrance, but it doesn't equal in size or in beauty the Lemonade River, which likewise empties into Lake Almond Milk."

And indeed, Marie soon heard a louder plashing and splashing and she spotted the broad Lemonade River. In proud, cream-colored waves, it rippled away amid green-glowing, garnet-shining shrubs. An exceeding freshness, cooling her breast and her heart, surged up from the

The Kingdom of Dolls

stunning water. Not too far from there, the water of a dark yellow creek was being arduously dragged away, spreading utterly sweet perfumes. On the shore, all kinds of very lovely little children sat angling small, thick fish and consuming them right away. Upon coming closer, Marie noticed that these fish looked like hazelnuts.

In the distance, a very pretty hamlet lay on the creek: houses, church, parsonage, barns—they were all dark brown, but decorated with gold roofs. Furthermore, countless walls were painted so colorfully as if lemon peels and almond kernels were pasted on them.

"That's Gingerbreadhome," said Nutcracker. "It lies on Honey River and it's inhabited by very lovely people. But they're mostly grouchy because they suffer terribly from toothaches. That's why we're not going inside."

At that moment, Marie noticed a pretty little townlet consisting of colorful, transparent cottages. Nutcracker headed straight in that direction, and now Marie heard a wild, joyful uproar. She also saw a thousand sweet little people examining and starting to unpack many crammed wagons standing in the marketplace. But what they produced was gaudy, colored paper and bars of chocolate.

"We're in Bonbonville," said Nutcracker. "A shipment has just arrived from Paper Land and from Chocolate King. A short while ago, the poor Bonbonvillers were harshly threatened by Mosquito Admiral's navy. That's why they've covered their homes with the gifts of Paper Land and why they're constructing proficient works sent them by Chocolate King. However, dearest Demoiselle Stahlbaum, we don't plan to visit every last townlet and hamlet of this land. To the capital! To the capital!" Nutcracker rushed forward and Marie, filled with curiosity, brought up the rear.

It wasn't long before the fragrance of roses wafted up, and everything was surrounded by a gentle, floating shimmer of roses. Marie perceived that this was the image in a rosy red shining creek, which flowed in tiny pink and silver waves, gushing and rushing as if in wondrously beautiful notes and melodies. On this graceful water, which broadened out more and more like a huge lake, marvelous silver white swans with golden neckbands were swimming and vying with one another in singing the loveliest songs. Tiny diamond fish emerged and submerged, as if dancing a merry dance on the floods of roses.

"Ah!" cried Marie enthusiastically. "Ah! This is the lake that Godfather Drosselmeier wanted to make for me, truly, and I myself am the girl who will caress the dear little swans."

Nutcracker smirked more scornfully than Marie had ever noticed on him. Then he said: "That's something that Uncle will never be able to do. You will manage to do so yourself, dear Demoiselle Stahlbaum. But let's not ponder it too deeply. Instead, let's cross the Lake of Roses and head for the capital."

THE CAPITAL

Nutcracker clapped his tiny hands again, and the Lake of Roses started rushing more and more strongly, the waves splashing higher and higher. Marie noticed a shell-shaped vehicle coming from far away and drawn by two dolphins covered with golden scales. The vehicle was formed by gaudy, sunny, and sparkling jewels. Twelve darling little Moors, wearing caps and loincloths woven out of shiny hummingbird feathers, sprang ashore. They carried first Marie, then Nutcracker, gently gliding over the waves to the vehicle, which then sailed across the lake. Oh, how lovely it was to see Marie in the rolling vehicle, surrounded by the fragrance of roses, flowing around the waves of roses. The two golden dolphins raised their nostrils and spurted crystal rays high in the air; and where the arcs fell flickering and twinkling, it sounded like the crooning of two fine and graceful voices.

"Who swims in the rosy lake? For goodness' sake! Midges, no bridges! Bmm, bmm, fish! What a dish! Hmm, hmm, swans, where are ponds? Swa, swa, goldbird! Trara—streams, reams, teams, beams! Angels, angels! Sing in wings!"

However, the twelve little Moors, who had sprung in back of the chariot, seemed to take the singing of the streams of water amiss. For they shook their parasols so hard that the date leaves they were made of got creased and crumpled! They also stamped their feet to a bizarre beat! "Clap and clip and clip and clap, to and fro! Moors dance a round, make a sound! Stir, fish, stir, swans. Drone, chariot, drone. Clap and clip and clip and clap, to and fro!"

"Moors are such merry people," said Nutcracker, somewhat embarrassed. "Goodness, you'll make the entire lake rebellious!" And indeed, a confusing uproar of wonderful voices exploded. They seemed to swim in the lake and in the air. But Marie ignored them all. Instead, she peered at the waves of fragrant roses, and each wave smiled back at her smiling girlish face—a graceful and a gracious face.

"Ah," cried Marie, joyfully clapping her little hands together. "Ah! Just look, dear Herr Drosselmeier! Princess Pirlipat is down there, smiling at me so wondrously and graciously. Oh, do look, Herr Drosselmeier!"

But Nutcracker sighed almost lamentably and said: "Oh, dearest Demoiselle Stahlbaum, that's not Princess Pirlipat—that's you and always you yourself. That's always your own gracious face smiling so dearly out of every billow of roses."

Marie threw back her head, shut her eyes tight, and was very ashamed. That same instant, she was lifted from the chariot by the twelve Moors and carried ashore. She now found herself in a small grove that was almost lovelier than Christmas Forest—since everything in it shone and sparkled. But especially, one could admire the strange fruit that hung from all the trees—fruit that was not only strangely colored but also marvelously fragrant.

"We're in Jellygrove," said Nutcracker, "and there's the capital."

What did Marie catch sight of now? How, you children, will I even start to describe the beauty and splendor of the city that spread out over a rich, flowery pasture before Marie's very eyes? Not only were the walls and towers resplendent in the most fantastic colors but, in regard to the forms of the houses, there was nothing similar anywhere in the world. For, instead of roofs, the houses had delicately pleated wreaths, and the towers were topped with the finest and most colorful foliage that could be seen.

When they passed through the gates, which looked as if they were built out of macaroons and frosted fruit, silver soldiers presented their rifles, and a manikin in a brocaded robe threw his arms around Nutcracker and said: "Welcome, dearest Prince, welcome to Jamburg!"

Marie was astonished that young Drosselmeier was addressed as Prince by a noble gentleman. But now she heard so many very fine voices bursting through one another, exulting and laughing for joy, playing and singing, that she couldn't think of anything else. Instead, she asked little Nutcracker just what it all meant.

"Oh, dearest Demoiselle Stahlbaum," replied Nutcracker, "it's nothing unusual. Jamburg is a merry, populous city, every day is like this. But let's keep going, please."

No sooner had they walked a few paces than they reached the great marketplace, which offered the most thrilling view. The surrounding houses were shuttered by sweets, gallery was piled on gallery; and at the middle there stood a high, frosted layer cake as the obelisk. All about it, four very artful fountains spewed orgeat, lemonade, and other superb sweet drinks aloft. And the basin filled up with cream, which could have been spooned out right away.

But lovelier than anyone else were the little people. Thousands of them crowded through, head by head, exulting and laughing and joking and singing. In short: they raised the merry uproar that Marie had already heard far away. There were elegant ladies and gentlemen, Greeks and Armenians, Jews and Tyroleans, officers and soldiers and preachers and shepherds and buffoons—in short: every kind of person to be found in the entire world.

In one corner the tumult increased, the crowd streamed apart. Then the Grand Mogul was carried across on a palanquin, escorted by ninety-three grandees and seven hundred slaves. But what happened was that in the other corner, the fish guild, some five hundred heads strong, was holding its parade. And it was also dreadful that the Turkish Grandee had the idea of riding across the marketplace with three thousand Janissaries followed by the huge pageant of the opera The Interrupted Sacrificial Feast—just as the crowd charged toward the layer cake, singing and beating their drums: "Up! Thank the powerful sun!" What pushing and shoving and driving and squealing! Soon there was also a lot of yammering! For a fisherman had lopped off a Brahman's head in the mob, and the Grand Mogul was nearly run over by a buffoon.

The racket grew wilder and wilder, and the participants were already starting to lunge into one another and beat one another, when the man in the brocade robe climbed up the layer cake. This was the man who had greeted Nutcracker as Prince. Now, after a very dazzling bell was pealed three times, he cried aloud three times: "Confectioner! Confectioner! Confectioner!"

The tumult promptly faded, and each man tried to help himself as best he could. After the entanglements were untangled, the filthy Grand Mogul was cleaned and brushed, and the Brahman's head was put back on again. And now the merry clamor resumed.

"What's all this about the Confectioner, my good Herr Drosselmeier?" asked Marie.

"My dearest Demoiselle Stahlbaum," replied Nutcracker. "'Confectioner' is our name for an unknown but very ghastly power that we believe can do whatever we like to a human being. It is the doom hanging over this small, cheerful nation. And this little nation is so frightened that the mere mention of its name can silence the loudest tumult, as was just proved by the mayor. Each man then stops thinking about earthly matters, about pokes in the ribs and bumps on the head. Instead, he draws into himself and says: 'What is man and what can become of him?'"

Marie couldn't help crying out in loud admiration, nay, supreme amazement. She was suddenly standing in front of a rose red brightly shimmering castle with a hundred airy turrets. But now and again, rich bouquets of violets, narcissi, tulips, and gillyflowers were scattered on the walls; and the dark, burning colors simply dazzled as they heightened the rosy tint against the white ground.

The Capital

The vast dome of the central building as well as the pyramid-shaped roofs of the turrets were strewn with a thousand gold and silver twinkling stars. "Now we're outside the Marzipan Castle," said Nutcracker.

Marie was totally absorbed in viewing the enchanted palace, but it did not escape her that the roof of one huge tower was completely missing. Small manikins, perching on a scaffold of cinnamon sticks, appeared intent on restoring the rooftop. Before managing to ask Nutcracker about it, he continued:

"A short while ago, this beautiful castle was threatened with destruction if not total devastation. Sweet-Tooth the Giant came along, quickly bit off that roof, and was already gnawing on the huge dome. However, the Jamburgers brought him an entire city district plus a considerable section and a confect grove as a tribute, which he fed on and then went his way."

At that same moment, a very gentle and pleasant music could be heard, the gates of the castle opened up, and twelve little pageboys came out, holding clove stems like torches in their little hands. A page's head consisted of a pearl, his body of rubies and emeralds, and they walked about on little feet beautifully worked in pure gold. They were followed by four ladies almost as big as Marie's Clärchen, but so elegantly shining and splendid that Marie could not mistake the born princesses in them for even an instant. She embraced Nutcracker tenderly and exclaimed with mournful joy:

"Oh, my prince! My dearest prince! Oh, my brother!"

Nutcracker seemed deeply moved. He wiped the dense tears from his eyes, took hold of Marie's hand, and spoke grandiloquently:

"This is Demoiselle Stahlbaum, the daughter of a very highly appreciated medical counselor and the savior of my life. If she hadn't hurled the slipper at the right time, if she hadn't gotten me the sword of the retired lieutenant, then I'd be lying in the grave, all chewed up by that accursed Mouse King!

"Oh! That Demoiselle Stahlbaum! Does she equal Pirlipat in beauty, kindness, and virtue, even though she is a born princess? No, I tell you, no!"

And all the ladies cried: "No!" And they hugged Marie and they sobbed: "Oh, you savior of the beloved princely brother—excellent Demoiselle Stahlbaum!"

Now the ladies escorted Marie and Nutcracker into the interior of the castle, a vast space whose walls consisted of colorfully sparkling crystals. But what Marie liked best of all were the darling little chairs, tables, dressers, secretaries, which stood around. They were made of cedar and brazilwood with golden blossoms scattered upon them. The princesses urged Marie and Nutcracker to have a seat, and they themselves would prepare a meal! They pulled out a lot of little pots and bowls made of the finest Japanese porcelain—and knives and spoons and forks and grates and casseroles, and other kitchen appliances of gold and silver. Then they brought the loveliest fruits and sweets, such as Marie had never seen before, and then they tenderly squeezed the fruits with their tiny white hands, pounded the spices, and grated the sugar almonds. In short, they knew their way around a kitchen. And the princesses could see that they were preparing a delicious meal.

While vividly feeling that they likewise understood such things, Marie secretly desired that she could be actively present at the activities of the princesses. As if she had read his mind, Nutcracker's most beautiful sister handed Marie a small gold mortar, saying: "Oh, sweet friend, dearest savior of my brother, grind me a wee bit from this rock candy!" Marie pounded away so cheerfully that the mortar resounded, graceful and charming, like a lovely tune.

Nutcracker started telling his tale—indeed, sprawling and rambling. He told about the gruesome battle between his army and Mouse King's army, about his losing due to the cowardice of his troops. Nutcracker also told about how the repulsive Mouse King wanted to chew him to bits; and Marie therefore had to sacrifice a few of the subjects in her service.

During this narrative, Marie felt as if her words, nay, her pestle strokes were moving farther away, growing hazier and hazier. Soon, rising like flimsy clouds of mist, Marie watched the silvery gauzes, in which the princesses, the pageboys, and Nutcracker swam. They could hear a bizarre singing and whirring and whizzing, which vanished in the distance. And now Marie wanted to ascend as if surging on billows, higher and higher, higher and higher, higher and higher.

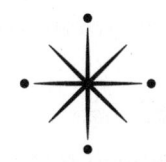

CONCLUSION

"Prr! Puff!" resounded. Marie plunged down from an immeasurable height. Now that was a jolt! She opened her eyes and found herself lying in her little bed. It was broad daylight, and her mother stood in front of her, saying: "How can anyone sleep so long? Breakfast has been ready for quite a while."

Highly esteemed audience! You do notice that Marie, utterly dazed by all the wonders she had seen, had finally dozed off in the vast hall of Marzipan Castle. Next, she had been carried home and put to bed by the Moors or the pages or even the princesses themselves.

"Oh, Mother, dear Mother! Where did the young Herr Drosselmeier take me to last night, and what gorgeous things did I see?!" Now Marie told me everything almost as precisely as I just did. And [Mother] gaped at her in amazement.

When Marie was finished, Mother said: "You've had a very long and very lovely dream, dear Marie. But now you've simply got to dismiss all such thoughts from your mind."

However, Marie obstinately insisted that she hadn't been dreaming, that she had really seen all those things. Mother then led her to the glass cabinet, took out Nutcracker from his usual place on the third shelf, and said: "You silly girl! How can you truly believe that this wooden Nuremberg doll can have life and motion?"

"But Mother dear!" Marie broke in. "I do know that little Nutcracker is young Herr Drosselmeier's nephew from Nuremberg!"

Both parents burst into noisy laughter.

"Ah," Marie went on almost tearfully. "Now you're actually making fun of my Nutcracker, Father dear, even though he spoke so highly of you. For when we arrived at Marzipan Castle, and Nutcracker introduced me to his sisters, the princesses, he said that you were a very respectable medical counselor!"

This time, the laughter, which now emerged from

Luise and even Fritz, was all the more vociferous. So Marie ran into the next room, quickly reached into her small casket, produced the seven crowns of Mouse King, and handed them to her mother, saying: "Just look, Mother dear! These are Mouse King's seven crowns, which young Herr Drosselmeier gave me last night as a sign of his victory!"

The astonished mother viewed the tiny crowns. They were worked so cleanly from a totally unfamiliar, but intensely sparkling metal that they couldn't have been wrought by human hands. Nor could the medical counselor see his fill of the little crowns. And both Father and Mother deeply urged Marie to reveal where she had obtained the crowns. But she could only stick to what she had said.

When her father started treating her severely, even scolding her and calling her a little liar, Marie burst into tears and lamented: "Ah, poor child that I am, poor child! What should I say now?"

At that moment, the door flew open. The Supreme Court counselor came in and exclaimed: "What's this? What's this? My dear little child weeping and sobbing? What's this? What's this?"

The medical counselor informed him about everything that had happened, and he showed him the little crowns. But no sooner had he seen the crowns than he laughed and said: "Empty twaddle! Empty twaddle! Why those are the little crowns I wore on my watch chain years ago!

I gave them to little Marie on her second birthday! Have you all forgotten?"

Neither the medical counselor nor his wife could remember. But when Marie saw that the faces of her parents had grown friendly again, she sprang upon Godfather Drosselmeier and exclaimed: "Ah! You know everything, Godfather! Just tell them that my Nutcracker is your nephew, the young Herr Drosselmeier from Nuremberg, and that he gave me the crowns."

But the Supreme Court counselor scowled and muttered: "Silly, mindless twaddle."

Thereupon, the medical counselor took little Marie before him and spoke very earnestly: "Listen, Marie. Forget about your antics and your fantasies! If you ever repeat that the deformed and simpleminded Nutcracker is the nephew of Herr Supreme Court Counselor, I'll hurl all your dolls out the window—not only Nutcracker but all your others, including Mamsell Clarchen!"

Now poor Marie could no longer talk about what her mind was filled with. For you can certainly imagine that Marie's lovely and splendid experiences were unforgettable. Even my highly esteemed reader or listener Fritz—even her comrade Fritz Stahlbaum turned his back on his sister when she tried to tell him about the miraculous realms where she was so happy. At times, supposedly, he had even muttered between his teeth: "Silly goose!"

Still, I can't believe he really said that, given his tried and tested disposition. This much, however, is certain:

Since Fritz no longer believed what Marie told him, he virtually apologized to his Hussars in public review; apologized for the injustice he had made them suffer. Instead of the lost ensigns, far higher and lovelier bushes of goose quills decorated them and again permitted them to blast the Hussar March. Well, we know best about the courage of the Hussars, when they got spots from their ugly dumplings on their red jerkins!

Though Marie was not allowed to talk about her adventures, the images of that wondrous fairyland hovered around her in sweetly rushing billows and gracious, charming sounds. She looked at everything once more, focusing sharply. And so, in lieu of playing as usual, she sat there, quiet and rigid and deeply self-absorbed. That is why everyone scolded her for being a little "dreamer."

Now one day, the Supreme Court counselor was repairing a clock in the medical counselor's home. Marie was sitting by the glass cabinet, deep in her dreams, and peering at Nutcracker. All at once, she blurted out: "Ah! Dear Herr Drosselmeier! If you were truly alive, I wouldn't treat you like Princess Pirlipat, scorning you because, for my sake, you stopped being a handsome young man!"

At that moment, the Supreme Court counselor yelled: "Hey! Hey! Empty twaddle!" At that instant, there was such a whack and boom that Marie fainted and sank from her chair.

When she awoke, her mother was busily attending to her and she said: "How can you fall from the chair—such a big girl! The nephew of the Supreme Court counselor has just arrived from Nuremberg. Be a good girl!"

Marie looked up. The Supreme Court counselor had put his glass periwig back on, slipped into his yellow jacket, and smiled in great satisfaction. His hand clutched a small, but very well-built young man, while his little face had a peaches-and-cream complexion. He wore a splendid red coat with a gilt lining, white silk shoes and stockings, and a darling bouquet in his jabot. He was also nicely groomed and powdered, and a wonderful queue hung down his back. The little sword on his side glittered as if thoroughly encrusted with jewels, and the cap he held under his arm seemed woven out of silk flocks.

The young man's pleasant habits were demonstrated immediately by the many gorgeous toys he had brought for Marie. He also offered her the most delectable marzipan and the same figurines that Mouse King had chewed up, whereby the young man had also gotten Fritz a magnificent saber.

During the meal, the well-behaved young man cracked nuts for the entire company. Not even the hardest shells could resist him. With his right hand, he inserted the nuts into his mouth; and with his left hand, he pulled his queue—crack! The nut fell into pieces!

Marie had turned bright red upon seeing the well-behaved young man.

And she turned even redder after the meal, when

young Drosselmeier invited her to join him at the glass cabinet in the living room.

"Play nicely with one another, children," the Supreme Court counselor exclaimed. "I don't mind playing now that all my clocks run correctly."

But no sooner was young Drosselmeier alone with Marie than he knelt down on one knee and said:

"Oh, my highly esteemed Demoiselle Stahlbaum! See at your feet your happy Drosselmeier, whose life you saved on this very spot! You were kind enough to state that if I grew ugly for your sake, you would not scorn me like that wretched Princess Pirlipat. I promptly stopped being a despicable Nutcracker and I regained my earlier, not unpleasant looks. Oh, highly esteemed Demoiselle! Delight me with your worthy hand. Share crown and kingdom with me, rule from Marzipan Castle with me, for I am now king there."

Marie lifted up the youth and said quietly:

"Dear Herr Drosselmeier! You are a kind and gentle person! And since you also rule a graceful land with very cheerful and attractive people, I will accept you as my fiancé!" Marie hereby became Drosselmeier's fiancée.

A year later, we are told, he called for her in a golden carriage drawn by silver horses. Twenty-two thousand of the most brilliant figurines danced amid their adornments of pearls and diamonds.

Marie supposedly is still queen of a land where you can see sparkling Christmas Forests everywhere as well as translucent Marzipan Castles—in short, the most splendid and most wondrous things, if you only have the right eyes to see them with.

And that was the tale of Nutcracker and Mouse King.